THE END OF PROJECT 38

THE END OF PROJECT 38

by

EDWIN JOHNSON

THE CHILDREN'S PRESS
LONDON AND GLASGOW

First printed 1963

CONTENTS

CHAPTER ONE

THE MISSION

WITH AN ear-splitting roar the demonstration shed exploded in a sheet of flames. The blast sent Merridew and Sherwood sprawling, with showers of debris about their ears.

As they lay, still half dazed, the smoke thinned enough to show that nothing remained but a steel skeleton and a heap of burning wreckage.

Then Merridew, who was the first to recover, launched himself forward, an automatic in his hand, in pursuit of the shadowy figure disappearing into the darkness on the far side of the gun park. Two shots came from the direction he had taken.

Sherwood staggered up and clung to the barrel of a captured German field-gun, his head ringing like a bell from the explosion. He was still there when help began arriving from the camp.

The Commandant, Brigadier Grey, ran over to him.

"Are you all right, Sherwood?"

He nodded uncertainly, wiping blood from cuts on his face.

"I've been hit by flying gravel, sir, but I'll be O.K."

"What happened? Did Project 38 just blow up by itself?"

"We saw someone throw a grenade through the window, then the whole place went up. Merridew's gone after him."

The Commandant looked grim.

"Some grenade," he said. "You'd better have your face attended to right away, then go back to your hut. I'll send for you later if I want you." He strode off towards the fire where a crowd was already gathering, leaving Sherwood with Colonel Nicholson, who had come down earlier in the day from the War Office with Merridew.

"Did you recognise the chap who threw the bomb, Sergeant?" demanded the Colonel.

"It was too dark and I saw him for only a second, sir."

The Colonel frowned.

"Must have been someone in this unit. It doesn't seem possible, though . . . anyone in the shed?"

Sherwood told him that all the investigating team had been in there.

"Poor devils. And the Resistance chap who smuggled Project 38 out of Belgium for us, was he there too?"

"Yes, I saw him going in, sir."

Colonel Nicholson smacked the gun-barrel angrily and turned away muttering, but what he said was lost in the noise of the fire-tenders and ambulances arriving from the School of Artillery at Larkhill.

The Commandant and Merridew pushed their way back out of the crowd.

"All dead, Nick," said the Commandant bitterly to Colonel Nicholson, "everything blown sky-high. Project 38 kaput, finished." He caught sight of Sherwood and added irritably: "I thought I told you to clear off, Sergeant."

Sherwood saluted hurriedly and turned away towards the living-quarters. Merridew fell into step beside him.

"The blighter got away. There was too much smoke about and he gave me the slip. The camp is completely sealed, so he can't escape. How are you feeling? I was a bit behind you and you must have sheltered me from the blast." He looked doubtful when Sherwood said that he was all right. "Better clean your face up, anyhow—I'll come with you. There are one or two things I want to talk to you about."

As Sherwood led the way across the camp, the flames behind them were reflected from low clouds and the dense smoke rolling away across Salisbury Plain.

Sherwood's bunk consisted of part of a Nissen

hut, which had been partitioned off to make quarters for six sergeants. Merridew hitched up his neat, pin-striped trousers and perched himself on the bed. He inspected the room while Sherwood combed pieces of gravel out of his unruly red hair and stripped off for a shower.

"So this is how the Army lives," he remarked. "Can't say I'd care for it much myself. Tell me, laddie, what exactly is done in this unit?"

Sherwood was rather puzzled at this, because he had put Merridew down as one of the civilian scientists who frequently came from the Ministry of Supply in London to look over the more important German weapons being investigated. Early in 1944 Resistance groups on the Continent were smuggling these weapons out to Britain in great numbers. But when Sherwood came to think of it, Merridew seemed remarkably fit for a chair-borne Civil Servant and he had been pretty fast with his automatic, too. He was a good deal slimmer than the stocky Sherwood, but with a tough, whip-lash slimness. It seemed rather odd that he was not in the Services. He looked about twenty-three or -four—a bit older than Sherwood—and most people of that age were in uniform.

He must have guessed what Sherwood was thinking, for he laughed. "Don't look so worried. Colonel Nicholson brought me down so that I could get some idea of what went on here. I work for him, you know."

Sherwood had not known, but it seemed a fair enough explanation so, while patching up the cuts on his face, he told Merridew what was being done at the Royal Artillery Investigation of Enemy Ordnance Unit on Salisbury Plain. The main jobs were to see if the captured weapons contained ideas which could be used by the Allies and also to find out what special precautions were necessary to counteract the enemy's technical advances.

"Sounds very complicated," said Merridew wryly. "Where do you fit into this picture?"

"I was training to be a journalist before the war," Sherwood told him, "so I'm used now on preparing reports for the Supply Ministry and the Imperial General Staff and I do a bit of interpreting, too."

Merridew nodded. "Yes, I know. You were born in Belgium, weren't you?"

This made Sherwood stare, but before he could ask how Merridew knew about that, an orderly came in to say that the Commandant wanted them both in his office.

"Come on, we'd better not keep him waiting," said Merridew, slipping off the bed. He produced his automatic and grinned. "Just in case, you know! There are some rough characters about."

In spite of what had happened to the demonstration shed, Sherwood could not believe that it was necessary to march across the camp, gun in hand, and told Merridew so. " After all," he said, "lightning never strikes twice in the same place."

"Don't be too sure, laddie," Merridew replied. "Black lightning does. You can depend on it."

It was not until much later that Sherwood realised he had been referring to the insignia of the *Schutzstaffel* or S.S., Hitler's fanatical Nazi guard. However, they reached the Commandant's office without incident and found him waiting impatiently with Colonel Nicholson.

The Colonel had hunched himself up in the corner by the stove and was noisily sucking an empty pipe. He looked inquiringly at Merridew as they came in and Sherwood noticed that Merridew nodded as though in answer to a question.

" Sit down, you two," snapped the Commandant irritably and turned to the Colonel. "This is all quite beyond me, Nick. This is your sort of game. What happens next?"

"Next?" growled the Colonel. "First of all—what's happened already? One: your demonstration-shed is blown up together with a very interesting new German weapon. Two: after the camp is sealed off, we shoot Bombardier Hynes who is trying to get out through the security fences and won't stop when challenged. . . ."

Sherwood pricked up his ears at that. He knew Hynes, an N.C.O. in charge of one of the mess halls.

"That was ridiculous," burst out the Commandant angrily. "Hynes was perfectly harmless. He's been here for over two years."

"Was he, though?" said the Colonel. "Let me tell you something about Master Hynes: we'd known about him for some time. Every week he went into Salisbury, had tea and then went to the cinema—always the same cinema. When he left, he stopped to chat with the Commissionaire for a few minutes and sometimes passed him a piece of paper. A progress report on your work up here."

"And you let him do it?" exploded the Commandant. "It—it was . . ." He caught sight of Sherwood and did not finish what it was.

"Well, you know," continued the Colonel unruffled. "It didn't get very far. The Commissionaire was one of our chaps. Hynes didn't know that, of course, and the messages we passed on to the Jerries were not the ones he prepared—see what I'm getting at?"

"Yes, I suppose so," said the Commandant doubtfully. "But why couldn't you have passed the faked messages on without leaving Hynes loose?"

"I'm coming to that," said the Colonel patiently. "Hynes received his instructions from someone in London whom he used to meet when on leave. A big fish and a slippery one. We picked him up this morning; and now we've got Hynes into the bargain. Your Bombardier Hynes belonged to the *Sicherheitsdienst*, the export model of the S.S. A little villain, but a nasty one."

"You left it a bit late," snapped the Commandant darkly. "There may be no Hynes, but there's no Project 38 either, and five of my chaps have been killed as well."

"I'm desperately sorry," replied the Colonel, "but I had no idea that anything like this was on the cards. Hynes was a sneaker of bits of information, and not up to much at that. We were checking to see what other contacts he had made before bringing him in. But now there's something more important to think about: Project 38 and Sergeant Richard Sherwood here."

"Don't tell me that Sherwood's a Nazi Agent too," shouted the Commandant. "What has he been up to? Is my unit just a nest of spies, Nick?"

The Colonel smiled briefly, then took a dossier out of his document-case.

"Nothing like that," he said soothingly. "I just want to check my records." He turned to Sherwood: "Now, tell me if I have missed anything out or got anything wrong."

Then, to Sherwood's astonishment, the Colonel started reading out his life history. It went right back to his school-days in Belgium and covered in accurate detail the export firm his father had worked for, all the addresses at which his family had lived, even that they had always spent their holidays fishing and hunting in the Ardennes. The Colonel knew about the newspaper on which Sherwood had been a very junior reporter before the war—in fact he knew things that Sherwood himself had forgotten.

He must have looked as staggered as he felt because Merridew leaned forward and tapped his knee.

"It's all done with mirrors, laddie," he murmured. "The quickness of the hand deceives the eye."

"All correct, Sherwood?" asked the Colonel when he had finished.

"All correct, sir."

"Right," he said, turning to the Commandant. "Now about his technical qualifications. Would you say that Sherwood is really well-informed about artillery?"

The Commandant nodded suspiciously. "For an amateur he's well up in the latest developments. He has been on the basic rocketry course. Yes, he has a good grasp of what is going on," he said. "Why?"

Merridew grinned at Sherwood and silently applauded. The Colonel frowned at him before continuing: "We've had information that Project 38 is being given top priority by the Germans. They have sealed off, with security cordons, a great area in the south of Belgium for it, and we know that their best ballistic experts have been transferred there, even though that must mean putting off work on other important weapons. I've seen your preliminary reports on the specimen you've had here. From your accounts, it is a small rocket with retractable fins, nothing to get very excited about. And yet the Jerries are prepared to sacrifice Hynes, whom they must have thought was a useful agent, to destroy the sample that came into our hands. They've never tried anything like that before. It all goes to confirm a hunch I've had. We may have stumbled on one of the biggest secrets of the war."

"Well, what has that to do with where Sherwood went to school?" snapped the Commandant. He was obviously a bit annoyed about the implied criticism of his technical reports.

"Well, I need a reliable man who knows about guns, can speak French and Flemish like a native," said the Colonel. "I need him to go to Belgium and find out what Project 38 really is." He swung round. "Sherwood, you fit the bill—will you go?"

CHAPTER TWO

SPECIAL OPERATIONS H.Q.

SHERWOOD ROLLED off the bed and pulled back the blackout curtain. The position of the wintry sun showed that he had slept until nearly midday, which was not surprising since there had been little time for rest the previous night.

After he had agreed to Colonel Nicholson's suggestion that he should go to Belgium, the Colonel had insisted on an immediate return to London and within an hour they were speeding across Wiltshire in a civilian Humber expertly driven by Merridew.

On reaching the city the Colonel said there was urgent business for him in Whitehall and left them to carry on to their destination, which turned out to be a large house in Hampstead.

Merridew drove straight into the garage and shut the doors before letting Sherwood out.

"Just for the neighbours, laddie," he grinned. "They might be upset if they saw a rough soldier in uniform arriving in the middle of the night."

A side door gave directly from the garage on to the hall of the house and once inside Sherwood soon realised that they were in some sort of under-cover headquarters. He noticed, too, that the armed civilians guarding the doors gave Merridew a pretty respectful greeting.

"Room Two is ready for the Sergeant, sir," one of them called. "And your usual for you."

"Good. We'll be turning in right away. Send up something hot to drink, there's a good chap."

Merridew led the way upstairs and pointed to a door marked "No. 2."

"Home from home for Special Operations Branch. You'll find it neat but not gaudy. Spies boarded at special rates, laddie. Good night."

He was right, the room was plainly furnished, but the camp-bed was all Sherwood needed. Without waiting to undress, he flung himself down and was asleep within minutes.

Now, as he peered round the curtain, he saw that he was in an expensive neighbourhood. Large, red-brick houses stood well back at the end of gravel drives, screened from the road and each other by trees. At least, they would have been screened if there had been any leaves on the trees.

A glint of light caught his eye from the house opposite. Something winked like a small mirror reflecting the sunlight. Still half awake, he was just wondering if someone was signalling when he was jerked violently away from the window.

It was Merridew and he looked furious.

"What a fool I am not to have warned you," he snapped. "I should have told you not to do that. If you want to look out of the window without being seen, stand well back. Never peep around curtains. Let's hope no one saw you, especially in that—" he nodded at Sherwood's crumpled battle-dress. "I've brought you some civvies. Change into them as quickly as you can, then nip into the room opposite. When they've finished with you there, come next door. We'll be waiting."

Then he was gone, leaving Sherwood wondering what the fuss was about. After all, they were still in England and there were enough men around in khaki for the sight of one looking out of a window to be commonplace. But then he remembered how Merridew had smuggled him in by the side door during the night and realised that these precautions might be more necessary than he had thought.

Merridew had left on the bed a change of well-worn clothing, complete right down to socks and handkerchief. They were the clothes of a Belgian outdoor worker, with the Continental maker's labels still attached.

When Sherwood had put them on he went into the room opposite and found a photographer waiting to take pictures, which he said were for fake identity papers and passes. He went over every detail of Sherwood's appearance.

"You'll do, I think," he said at length, "but before I take the photos you'll have to wash that grease out of your hair. There aren't enough fats in Belgium to make fancy hair-cream—not for a working chap like you'll be, at any rate."

This sort of thoroughness was reassuring, at least it was until he added that special precautions were being taken since agents sent to Holland had been disappearing without trace.

Cheered by his information, Sherwood went to the next room, where Merridew was talking with Colonel Nicholson and another man, both in civilian clothes.

The Colonel waved Sherwood to a chair and stared at him gravely across the table.

"Now, Sherwood, I want you to listen very carefully to a few simple instructions, because your life and Merridew's may well depend on them."

"Merridew's, sir?" queried Sherwood. It was the first he had heard of Merridew going with him.

"Yes, you will be going to Belgium with Merridew. He will get you to the Ardennes and your job will be to provide the technical knowledge for a thorough examination of Project 38. It's not an ideal arrangement and we don't usually work like this, but there's no time to give you the training which most agents have."

Sherwood glanced curiously at Merridew and caught a faint grin in return. The Colonel must have noticed the glance, because he broke off.

"I'm sorry, Sherwood," he said, "I haven't properly introduced you two, have I? Peter Merridew here, is one of the most unscrupulous, insubordinate, but efficient agents we have in Special Operations Branch, which is our organisation for waging undercover war in enemy-occupied territory. He's been parachuted three times into France and twice into Belgium and if he's been as much of a nuisance to the Germans as he has been to me, the war is as good as won!"

Merridew's grin broadened.

"That's pure libel, laddie. There's nothing to it, really. Just grow a beard and cultivate an innocent expression underneath. You can't go wrong."

"Never mind about that," growled the Colonel, "the point is that you will be going as a team. It's no secret, is it, that we and the Americans will be invading Europe in a few months? We must know well in advance if the Jerries are developing new weapons to meet us with. And there's not a minute to lose. The success of the invasion, the lives of thousands of Allied soldiers and the outcome of the war may all depend on what you two can find out."

It all sounded so impressive that Sherwood wondered whether he was the right chap for the job; but the Colonel pressed on:

"I'm not going to tell you more than is necessary, because the less you know the better for you and everyone else. Major Burke here"—he nodded at the stranger—"will brief you about your identity and the cover-story you're to tell if you're caught. Just before you leave he'll give you an address, to memorise in Charleroi, which you may go to only in an emergency.

"The general position is that our overseas organisations have been penetrated by the Nazis in both Belgium and Holland. Quite frankly, with one or two exceptions like our friend at Charleroi, we no longer know whom we can trust and whom we can't. We're sending agents to set up an entirely new network, but that's not your worry because you're to trust no one, except as I tell you.

"Your first job is to find the Resistance worker who stole the sample of Project 38 from the Ardennes. He was wounded getting out of the sealed area. That's why he couldn't come to England himself. He's being hidden somewhere near Ostend by the Resistance. I shall put you in touch with them. You will find out what you can about the installation from him and then— it's up to you two. I shall give details of your contacts, radio-operator and so on, to Merridew only, so if you lose him, Sherwood, make a break for Charleroi. If he can, he'll pick you up there. If not, you'll be sent on an escape route back home. Any questions so far?"

He paused for a moment, until Sherwood shook his head, then pushed a dossier across the table. Inside were some photographs clipped to several, typed foolscap sheets, which Sherwood recognised as one of his unit's preliminary technical reports on a captured, enemy weapon.

The photographs showed a rocket standing on its base with a scale indicating that it was eighteen inches long. A rod-like aerial projected from the nose for another six inches making the overall length two feet. The most unusual feature was a series of spring-loaded fins, which on one of the photographs were shown completely retracted into the body of the rocket. There was also a blown-up detail of a self-locking device designed to prevent the fins retracting once they had been fully extended.

The third photograph showed the rocket cut in halves lengthways so that the interior was revealed. The warhead, which was empty, was sprung against shock and there was a note stating that the interior and nose cap had been painted bright yellow.

"That dossier is all we have on Project 38," said

the Colonel when Sherwood looked up. " I want you to study it when we've finished here. It doesn't add up to much, as you'll see when you look at the report, but . . ."

"Hold it, sir!" said Merridew tersely. He was standing with his back to the fireplace staring across the room out of the window. "There's someone watching this place with binoculars from the nursing home opposite. I can see the sun reflected on the lenses."

The Colonel snatched a revolver and a pair of field-glasses from the table drawer and went over beside Merridew.

"I knew it was time to quit this place," he growled, focusing his glasses. "Burke, get some chaps over there at the double!"

Major Burke shot out of the room as the Colonel came back to the table to grab the telephone. Merridew took the field-glasses.

"He's got a camera—I can see it!" he shouted. "You know what that means—he's been photographing everyone he can see here. The Jerries'll have a complete record of us all, if we don't get him."

Sherwood remembered the flashing he had seen when looking out of the bedroom window. It was poor comfort to think that the secret photographer must have been facing into the sun. If he had managed to take a snap Sherwood knew that there would be less than a dog's chance in Belgium.

A door slammed below and several people ran down the drive towards the road.

"He spotted Burke," yelled Merridew, and darting across to the window, flung it open. His automatic slithered into his hand. He took careful aim and fired once—twice—three times. There was a distant tinkling of glass and a faint yell.

The Colonel and Sherwood looked over his shoulder. Major Burke and three other men were dodging frantically across the road between a bus and an oil tanker. They had to wait for some cars coming the other way before finally dashing into the drive opposite. As they did so, the dark shape of a low-slung saloon slid between the bushes and bore down on them. They barely had time to leap aside as it snarled in a wide skid out into the road. Sherwood made out two figures in the back, and glimpsed a swarthy, heavy face staring up at him as the car accelerated away. He knew that he would remember that face if ever he saw it again.

The Colonel grunted and put his hand out to stop Merridew firing again as the car disappeared into the traffic.

"Too many people about," he said absently. He seemed to be thinking about something else already and ignored Merridew's disgusted expression.

"I could have picked off a tyre, or the petrol tank, or something," muttered Merridew. "Couldn't miss at that range."

Major Burke came back breathlessly holding the shattered remains of a camera with a long lens.

"Good shooting, Merridew," he panted. "There's blood all over this thing, but the film's gone—might have been spoiled—but they took it all the same. It was one of the patients, sir—supposed to have had a nervous breakdown—left alone most of the time. The other two were visitors—arrived about an hour ago."

The Colonel nodded briefly, then looked at Merridew and Sherwood.

"Still prepared to go on with it? I can't pretend that this doesn't make a difference, and I certainly shouldn't blame you if you backed out."

Merridew shook his head. "I'm game," he replied, "but I wish I'd had a crack at that car. How about you, laddie?"

Sherwood nodded without saying anything. As a matter of fact, he could not think of anything to say.

"Good," said the Colonel, "I'm glad. Everything convinces me that we are playing for very high stakes. This morning while I was at the

Admiralty, the Prime Minister sent for me. He agreed that in view of the happenings of the past twenty-four hours, this investigation should have absolutely top priority, and he sent his best wishes to you both."

He held out his hand to Sherwood.

"I still have to give instructions to Merridew, but I shan't be seeing you again before you go. Major Burke will look after you until then. To-morrow night there'll be a submarine waiting for you at Harwich. You're sailing just after midnight. Good luck!"

CHAPTER THREE

TRAPPED IN OSTEND

SEVENTY-TWO HOURS later Merridew and Sherwood were in the conning-tower of H. M. Submarine *Finbow* wallowing in a rough sea some twenty miles off the Belgian coast.

They had been cruising around for nearly three hours waiting for the signal announcing the arrival of the fishing-boat which was to take them into Ostend.

Although the fresh air was welcome after the stuffy atmosphere of the cramped submarine, they were being alternately lashed by the icy wind and drenched by the sheets of spray thrown up as the heavy seas broke over the prow.

Merridew nudged Sherwood.

"You know the song about Drake being in his hammock and a thousand miles away—" he shouted, "—I wouldn't mind changing places with him for a cushy billet like that!"

Lieutenant Greer, commanding the *Finbow*, lowered his night-glasses and laughed.

"If you're worried by a refreshing breeze like this, you land-lubbers, it's just as well your bus is arriving to take you to land. It's just in time, too. I couldn't have hung around here much longer after the moon came up."

Sherwood peered in the direction he was pointing and saw a pinprick of light across the water.

The *Finbow* altered course and approached warily. There was always the chance that the rendezvous had been discovered and that they were heading towards a pack of German E-boats waiting to pounce and crush the life out of the submarine with depth-charges.

The forward gun had been uncovered and manned and was ready to go into action at the first suspicious sign, but after a few minutes the Lieutenant lowered his glasses again and said:

"You can get your gear together now, it's your trawler all right. I hope the skipper doesn't ram us. Some of these Belgian fishermen couldn't steer a pram."

He need not have worried for, as he took the *Finbow* up into the wind, a trawler with the registration letters "A.27" painted on its side, sidled out of the darkness into their lee and came expertly alongside.

"This is it, laddie," said Merridew, and Sherwood well understood the grimness in his voice. This would be the point of no return. Once aboard the trawler there would be no way back. Lieutenant Greer must have felt this, too, because he stepped back and saluted quite formally as they went over the side.

"Good luck!" he called.

"If anyone else wishes us good luck," grumbled Merridew, "I'll begin to believe we need it."

Their rucksacks were slung up on a line to the trawler and they followed, using a short rope-ladder. It was rather dodgy with the two ships sawing up and down side by side, but after a hectic scramble they were dragged safely on to the deck.

Sherwood looked back at the *Finbow*. It was the last bit of England they would be seeing for a long time, perhaps for ever. But there was little time to think about it before they were escorted to the skipper's cabin.

When A.27 had swung round and got under way the skipper came down and joined them. He was a Fleming, stout as a barrel, with scarlet features and cropped grey hair. He stood at the door of his cabin sizing them up. Apparently satisfied with them, he introduced himself as Paul Krunjes and produced a bottle and some glasses.

"Sit down, boys," he roared in rusty English, "I have to tell you what we do, but first a drink. It is polite, eh?"

It was well enough meant, but it required all their

courage to down the colourless liquid which tasted and felt like sulphuric acid.

Merridew winked at Sherwood and moved his glass away before Krunjes could refill it.

"We are grateful to you for picking us up at short notice like this, Skipper," he said. "What are your plans for getting ashore?"

Krunjes explained that he was out with a small fishing-fleet, which the Germans allowed in order to provide much-needed food for the Belgian people. But, there was an escort of E-boats and the next move was to slip back to the fishing ground before being missed.

"When we reach Ostend, you stay on board while we land the fish. Then, to-morrow night you will be smuggled out of the docks."

"Will you be getting us out?" asked Merridew.

Krunjes nodded.

"All my life I smuggle things out of the docks," he chuckled. "Before the war it was my profession to smuggle. I am very good. You do not worry. Then I take you to my friend in the Resistance." He got up. "Now you have to hide before we rejoin the fleet. You like fish? Good! Because you must go down in the hold with the catch. Come—I show you." He led the way out along the deck.

There was no sign of the *Finbow*. She was no doubt already submerged. They were too close to the Belgian coast for her to lie safely on the surface in moonlight.

Krunjes looked anxiously up at the sky. He had left it pretty late. Already the sky was lightening with the full moon, which would increase the chance of their being spotted by the E-boats.

They followed him down the steel ladder into the hold and floundered over the fish to the rear bulkhead.

"Here you will hide until I tell you," he said, tugging back a hinged panel in the steel plates to reveal a foul-smelling hole about two feet deep and four feet high. Merridew and Sherwood squeezed inside reluctantly. It was suffocating, and, judging by the racket, they were just in front of the engine-room.

"You will be safe, unless there is a special search," boomed Krunjes encouragingly. He peered in at them and then roared with laughter. "You are comfortable, eh? Or perhaps you rather go home now."

What with the noise of the engine and the mixed smell of coal-dust and fish, Sherwood could not see anything to laugh about at the time, and neither apparently could Merridew.

"The next time I'll walk," he yelled, which pleased Krunjes no end.

The reverberations of the engine and the drumming of the steel plates were deafening and to take his mind off the row Sherwood tried to concentrate on going over the instructions which Major Burke had given to him in London.

He had forged identity papers and passes in the name of "Michel Richard," an electrical engineer from Ostend travelling to a new job in the mines near Charleroi. Major Burke had built up a complete character round Sherwood's family and pre-war background in Brussels, so that any reasonable question could be answered without hesitation. He had been satisfied that Sherwood would pass a routine questioning, but in case of arrest or interrogation under suspicion, he had thought up something else: after telling the first story Sherwood was to break down and admit that he had robbed his employers when their offices in Ostend had been bombed, and was making off with their pay-roll. To back this up, Sherwood had been given a roll of new Belgian notes with consecutive serial numbers, which looked as though they had just been drawn from the bank. There had been quite a lot of bomb damage in Ostend and the story would be difficult to check.

"People are more likely to believe you if you admit you're a crook," Burke had said. "We know —we've tried it. The Germans aren't very concerned about civil crimes and, if they believe you, will probably hand you over to the Belgian Police, many of whom are in the Resistance."

A Lüger automatic was strapped to the inside of Sherwood's left shin, where it would not be found unless there was a careful search. His rucksack contained nothing incriminating, only clothes, but Merridew was carrying some small explosive and incendiary devices disguised as pens and pencils. These would be explained by his assuming the identity of a French schoolmaster and, just to be on the safe side, he was carrying some books about Hitler's Nazi Party to show how friendly he felt towards the Germans.

Sherwood was trying to remember what his cover-name was supposed to be when the engine died away until it was just ticking over.

"We must be coming up with the other boats," said Merridew, "this will be the tricky part." But nothing alarming happened. The trawls were put out and A.27 started cruising up and down without interference.

It seemed endless in their funk-hole and Sherwood was just climbing out to stretch his legs when Merridew stopped him. "Listen!"

Faintly at first, but growing louder, the throb of a powerful motor came over the noise of their own engine. The rigging above lit up as it was caught in the beam of a searchlight, and the metallic sound of a voice amplified by a loud-hailer came across the water, but they could not make out what was said.

"It's one of the escorting E-boats. Probably giving the order to put back to Ostend," guessed Merridew.

He must have been right, for shortly afterwards the nets were brought in and discharged into the hold. Then the engine was speeded up until it felt as though it would shake A.27 to pieces.

Neither of them could stick the heat and noise for long, so they crawled out of the hole. But that was not much improvement, for they found themselves sliding around on the recently landed fish, many of which were still flapping about.

"Talk about the frying-pan and the fire!" shouted Merridew disgustedly, "To have the fish as well, that's too much! Let's go up on the deck. We don't have to show ourselves." But before they could do so, Krunjes appeared and slid down the ladder beside them.

"You get back, boys," he ordered, chuckling at their discomfort. "We're off Ostend now."

When they were in the hole again, even more reluctant than the first time, he thrust his face through the opening.

"You don't like this boat?" he grinned, "I tell you, I don't like her, too. I don't like her owner, also—he is a collaborator. One day I sink them both, eh?"

"Just invite me," said Merridew, "I'd like to be there!"

"But she is useful for the little jobs," said Krunjes with a shrug. Sherwood thought sourly that it was not difficult to imagine the sort of jobs he had in mind.

There was nothing else for it but to stick it out, and they were just stowing themselves as painlessly as possible when they heard the E-boat's motor coming up again, fast. This time it was much closer and when the loud-hailer opened up it sounded right alongside.

"A.27—A.27," it squawked. "You will pull over to quay Number Four for inspection. Do not—repeat NOT—proceed with the other boats to the inner basin."

Overhead, Krunjes was shouting a reply, but he was cut short by the metallic voice: "A.27—pull over to quay Number Four. You separated from the other boats during the night. You will be inspected."

Merridew reacted instantly: "Let's get out," he shouted, shoving back the steel panel. Krunjes had made it clear that, although the hiding-place would pass a casual inspection, it would not stand up to a thorough search. There was, therefore, no point in staying where they were. They swarmed up the ladder and met Krunjes coming to fetch them.

"You heard?" he demanded, "What do we do now? The *sales Boches*, they wait until we are back before they tell us. We cannot get away."

A glance was enough to confirm what he said. In the first grey light of day the quays of Ostend harbour showed up only a few hundred yards ahead. Behind, the other trawlers were being shepherded through the gap in the minefields by two sleek E-boats, while a third, the one which had hailed them, was close up to their stern, hugging their wash. They were completely trapped and within a few minutes would be inside the harbour.

"The only chance is for Sherwood and me to get ashore without being seen before we get to quay Number Four," said Merridew. "Can you cover us with smoke?"

Krunjes looked back at the E-boat and shook his head. "This is not possible. I cannot make enough smoke in time. I should have to set fire to the boat." He stared at them, struck by this idea. "Ja, I do that. I set fire to the boat! You shall have your smoke." He dashed off and disappeared down the companionway to the engine-room.

"Keep your eyes skinned for a likely place to land," said Merridew. "We must avoid a ducking if we can, otherwise we'll be too conspicuous when we're ashore."

They were already abreast of the light at the mouth of the harbour and could see that the quays were lined with ships, many of them damaged by bombing. There were no landing-stages in the few vacant spaces and the quay was too high to get up to from the deck of the trawler.

Then Sherwood spotted a place beyond a tanker where the quay had been heavily bombed and replaced by timber piling and temporary decking.

Merridew nodded when it was pointed out to him. "Ideal for our purpose if Krunjes can get us over there. We can hide under the decking until the row dies down," he agreed. "I'll get him." But, before he could reach the companionway, a man in overalls scrambled out, followed by Krunjes, who shot on to the deck yelling for everyone to get down.

Then A.27 seemed to stagger and leap into the air. A second later the hatches blew off and they had all the smoke they wanted. A thick, greasy cloud gushed from the engine-room to settle on the water and completely blot out the boats following. Several of the crew, thinking no doubt that the fuel tanks were going up, wasted no time in throwing themselves over the side.

Krunjes understood at once what was wanted, and ran to take the wheel himself. "You don't like my boat," he roared, "I sink her. I told you!"

In spite of the flames pouring up from the engine and the desperate position they were in, Sherwood could have sworn that Krunjes was enjoying himself as he wrestled to manœuvre them towards the piling. But whatever Krunjes himself was feeling, he was certainly spreading panic and dismay in the harbour. It did not occur to Sherwood until much later, but tankers are usually kept in special berths away from other ships due to their high fire risk. The one they were making for must have been heavily damaged for her to be tied up at a general quay. If she was damaged, then she was probably leaking and there was a very good chance that a spark from A.27 would turn the whole of Ostend harbour into an inferno. Krunjes must have known this, but it did not seem to bother him as they headed for the tanker's stern.

It was certainly bothering the Germans, though, for the E-boat following them swooped out of the smoke, her klaxon blaring, and tried to come alongside, between them and the tanker. Only by putting the wheel right over did Krunjes make her sheer off to avoid the danger of ramming the damaged vessel.

A.27, her engines now stopped, drifted completely round under the tanker's stern as the cloud of smoke, which had been trailing behind, caught up with them. Through it Sherwood saw the piling looming up, and yelled for Merridew. They had only a few seconds before A.27 would be carried on by the tide and her own momentum.

Merridew came running up behind. "Go on," he shouted. "Now!"

Sherwood balanced for one desperate second on the handrail and then crashed into the intersection of two massive timbers, hanging there completely winded by the impact and thinking of his rucksack still lying on the deck of the trawler.

Gingerly he hauled himself up to get one leg over the cross-piece. As there was no sign of Merridew, and the smoke was too dense to see whether he was still on A.27, Sherwood slid down towards the water to find out whether he had fallen in. Then he heard Merridew's voice, calling softly from high above, just under the decking.

"For Pete's sake get inside," hissed Merridew. "The smoke will clear in a minute and you'll look like the washing, hanging there!"

By the time Sherwood had struggled up to join him, the smoke was thinning and it was just possible to see across the harbour to where A.27 was drifting, out of control. The trawler's mast and rigging had collapsed across the E-boat and, in spite of the German crew's frantic attempts to free themselves, the fire had spread and both boats were blazing furiously.

"It's no use hanging about here," said Merridew, "we can't count on Krunjes being able to put us on to the Resistance. We'd better get out while everyone's watching the fireworks. We're in a spot now, all right!"

They climbed cautiously through the back of the decking to the top of the quay. There were several dockers about, but they were too intent on watching the death-struggles of the two boats to notice anything else.

"Make for the trucks—we'll hide there," said Merridew, pointing along the quay to a line of railway wagons. "With luck, they'll be already loaded and moving out of the docks soon."

But they were disappointed, for the wagons were still empty, which in one way was a good thing as the doors were not locked and they were able to slip inside without trouble. But this could be only a temporary hiding-place until loading started. Sherwood slid back the door facing over the harbour a few inches to see what was going on. There was a space of about thirty feet between the rails and the edge of the quay, so the view over the water was pretty restricted. What caught his eye right away was a group of black uniformed figures at the head of a flight of steps near a hut on which a large white figure "4" was painted.

He did not need Merridew to tell him that they were men of the S.S. They were living up to their brutal reputation, too, for they were beating up two of the crew of A.27 who had thrown themselves over the side when the fire started. The wretched fishermen must have been half drowned to start with, but that did not save them from the punches and kicks, which left them huddled, half-conscious, on the concrete.

The officer in charge, a bull-necked, white-faced man, was standing back, watching approvingly. He had rimless glasses and a small moustache which reminded Sherwood of someone.

"It makes your blood boil, doesn't it?" whispered Merridew fiercely. "Look at the beauty in charge of them! He's a pocket-size Himmler, all right."

That was whom he reminded Sherwood of, Himmler, the *Reichsführer* S.S.—the most feared man in Germany and Occupied Europe. There had been enough newspaper photographs to make the imitation easily recognisable. Sherwood was so fascinated by this first sight of the S.S. that when A.27 and the E-boat drifted through the smoke into view, he had almost forgotten their predicament.

By now both craft were burning down to the water-line, in spite of a fire-float which was pumping jets of water over them. At first they seemed to be abandoned, but then Krunjes appeared right up in the prow of the trawler, beating off attempts to drag him into a launch lying alongside. It was an unequal struggle, which could not last long. He wrenched himself free and stood outlined for a moment against the flames, before plunging forward into the water, dragging two of his attackers with him. The other boats closed round.

"Look—more boy scouts!" said Merridew, grimly, as a black van roared along the quay with S.S. standing on the running-boards.

The S.S. officer shouted to the driver of the van, who stopped and backed the vehicle up, until the rear was only a few yards from their hiding-place. The doors were flung open, giving them a good view of the interior, which consisted of a narrow central gangway with six or so compartments on either side, each just large enough to take a man standing.

The two fishermen, lying on the quay, were flung inside and locked in the compartments nearest the back, to an accompaniment of boos and cat-calls from Belgian dock-workers, who had been gathering round. They were promptly chased off with kicks and blows by the S.S., who then returned to the head of the steps to await the arrival of the launch carrying Krunjes.

Merridew tensed. "We must get Krunjes away from them. Come on, quickly! Follow me!"

To Sherwood's horror he slid down on to the quay and darted across to the back of the S.S. van and leapt inside, beckoning frantically.

Sherwood hesitated, quite convinced that Merridew had gone mad—then reluctantly followed him. Merridew shoved him down along the gangway to the compartments immediately behind the driver's cab.

"Get in there," he whispered fiercely, "pull the door to, but don't let it lock itself."

When Sherwood had done this, Merridew squeezed into the compartment opposite and, just as an uproar started outside, closed the door after him. Krunjes was apparently being landed. Sherwood could imagine the fight he was putting up and from the renewed booing of the dockers, the way it was ended. The skipper was dragged to the back of the van and bundled into a compartment next to one of his men. If he had been put farther up the van either Merridew or Sherwood would have been spotted and their game would have been up before it had started.

The doors were slammed and the van lurched off along the quay.

Well, they were in Belgium all right, reflected Sherwood grimly, in an S.S. van and on their way to an S.S. prison. Things might have turned out worse but, as they bounced along the rough *pavé* roads, it was difficult to imagine exactly how.

CHAPTER FOUR

KRUNJES'S HIDEOUT

ONCE CLEAR of the docks, Merridew wasted no time in setting about the doors of the compartments containing Krunjes and his two men, leaving Sherwood to keep watch on the inspection panel in the back of the driver's cab.

The chief danger was that one of the S.S. in front might take it into his head to see how the prisoners were getting on. But there was not much risk of that, as the only source of light was through the panel, which would have been blocked if anyone looked through it. It was not a very clever arrangement. The interior partitions were pretty flimsy and the locks gave Merridew little trouble. Obviously the S.S. expected no bother from prisoners once they had them aboard.

The two fishermen had not fully recovered from their beating, but Krunjes, although still dazed, was full of fight and came out of his compartment like a bull. He seized Merridew by the throat and half throttled him before realising who it was.

"This was a mistake," he chuckled, patting

Merridew's shoulder apologetically. "What we do now, boys, eh?"

"I can't open the rear doors, they're too tough and they're locked on the outside," croaked Merridew, feeling his throat painfully. "We shall have to persuade our chums up in front to open them for us. When I give the word, Sherwood, slide the inspection panel back and stick your gun into the officer's ear. Tell him to have the van pull into a side-street, then to give the key to the driver and to stay where he is until the rear doors have been opened for us. Tell him you'll blow his head off if there's any funny business—and if there is, laddie, do just that!" He crawled back to the rear doors and gave a thumbs-up sign.

Sherwood slid the glass panel aside and stuck the muzzle of his automatic against the fleshy neck of the S.S. officer. It was the same one who had been on the quay. Sherwood's German was not perfect, but the automatic helped to get the message across.

The van promptly pulled off the main road into an alley, and two minutes later the rear doors swung open to reveal the scared face of the driver. Krunjes leant out, dragged him inside and started stripping off his uniform, while his two ex-shipmates scuttled off down the alley and disappeared.

Sherwood could not see very well what was

happening because he was too occupied in keeping watch on the officer, who was getting a bit restive, wondering what his own fate would be. But he was not left in doubt long for the cab door snapped open and there was Merridew in the driver's cap and greatcoat, inviting him to come round to the back for the same treatment.

As the invitation was backed up by Merridew's automatic, it was accepted without argument and Krunjes went to work even more ferociously than on the driver. He was disappointed to find the uniform did not fit, so after extracting the identity papers, he tossed it aside.

"Well, *Hauptsturmführer* Bock," he roared, "let me return your hospitality," and banged the wretched German into the compartment he himself had just quitted, with a crash that nearly buckled the steel side of the van.

"Come up with me, Krunjes," called Merridew from the driver's cab. "Buck up, we haven't got all day."

Krunjes hurried round to join him while Sherwood kept a weather eye on the two prisoners. Some quick thinking was necessary. They could not hang around for long in Ostend, even in this deserted alley, without someone becoming curious. One thing was in their favour, as Sherwood soon found out: no one, not even the German troops, poked their noses into anything connected with the S.S. and the sinister black van proved to be a good cover. Even so, it would soon be missed and a search begun.

Merridew revved up the engine and accelerated out into the main road again, with the siren wailing. He drove as though on his way to a fire, ignoring police controls and forcing other traffic to make way.

His nerve paid off, for no one even tried to stop them, probably because they were so used to the S.S. behaving like that.

After twenty minutes or so they were clear of the town and running through the flat fields of Flanders. The first stop was to get rid of the prisoners. Krunjes appeared at the rear doors and dragged them out.

"Come, my dear sirs," he boomed, while he roughly blindfolded them, "you were so eager to see Belgium. Now you shall have a walk in our so-beautiful countryside. Come!"

He drove them out on to the road, across a ditch, into a field. A more wretched pair it would have been difficult to imagine as they stumbled blindly across the ploughed surface. They disappeared behind a small copse, urged on by the stentorian voice of Krunjes.

Merridew came round to the back, grinning broadly.

"Krunjes is taking us to a place where we can

lie low overnight," he said. "I think we ought to adopt him as our 'secret weapon.' The trouble would be keeping him secret. He's a bit on the loud side, isn't he?"

"What's he doing with them?" Sherwood asked doubtfully. It had occurred to him that once behind the trees Krunjes would not be above shooting them both out of hand. Merridew shrugged it off and went round to sound the hooter as a warning to Krunjes to hurry.

Krunjes was in great good humour when he returned, his red face beaming from ear to ear. Just as he was shutting the rear doors, the two Germans reappeared round the side of the copse. The plump officer was literally dancing with rage and screaming hysterically, but what he was saying was fortunately lost in the distance and he made no attempt to leave the shelter of the trees. The van started off again towards Ostend with Krunjes shouting and laughing in front. But on the whole, in spite of the lucky escape, there seemed to Sherwood little enough to laugh about.

In the outskirts of the town Krunjes directed Merridew to turn off along a deserted cinder-track between high banks. Once they were challenged and stopped briefly while Krunjes exchanged noisy greetings—then they moved on again in low gear.

When they finally halted, they were in a half-derelict barn among a group of disused farm-buildings perched on the bank of a broad dyke. Three farm-workers were waiting in the yard— at least they looked like farm-workers apart from the Sten guns and revolvers they were carrying and bandoliers of ammunition strapped across their shoulders. They welcomed Krunjes like a long-lost brother. There was much back-slapping and laughter; it was like a brigands' reunion.

"Are these the Resistance?" muttered Sherwood doubtfully.

Merridew grinned.

"No, not altogether. They're a mixture of Resistance, black market and any skulduggery that's going! They've picked themselves a pretty good hideaway here; a farm-house cut off from its land by the new dyke; only one road approach which a couple of men can easily control. It might have been designed for the job. Krunjes has been telling me about his smuggling before the war. These are some of his mates and this was one of his depots. We'll rest up here overnight before making contact with the genuine Resistance. They've sent a message through Krunjes where our 'cut-out' will be."

"Our 'cut-out'—what's that?"

"A contact man. Each Resistance group has a contact man who acts as go-between with other groups and outside agents like us. He will know only one man in the group he works for, so that if he is captured he can't give the whole group away. He's called a 'cut-out.' It's a risky job because he's the one the Germans are most likely to get on to."

He was interrupted by Krunjes, who, in high good humour, dragged them over to the farm-house.

"You eat," he said, "then sleep."

If anyone was going hungry in Belgium, it was certainly not Krunjes or his friends, for they had a larder well stocked with German rations.

Both Merridew and Sherwood had pretty healthy appetites, but compared with Krunjes they ate like gnats. He ate enough for six and swilled his food down with lavish draughts of red wine. After even he had finished, he took an oil-lamp and led the way to a room at the back of the building, where mattresses and palliasses were laid out on the floor. There he solemnly shook hands.

"You saved my life to-day. I shall not forget this," he said. "You sleep now. We will keep guard, do not worry. You will be safe." He put a sausage-like forefinger against his nose and winked. Then he disappeared out to the yard, leaving the lamp behind.

"What a character," grinned Merridew. "He may be useful to us, though. He's all right if you're a friend, but if not, you couldn't trust him an inch!"

"I know," Sherwood said drowsily. "I thought that he would kill those two Germans in cold blood this morning."

Merridew laughed. "What he did was almost as bad. He told them he was leaving them in the middle of an unmarked minefield. By the time they had their blindfolds off, he was too far off for them to follow. They're probably still standing there in their underclothes, afraid to put their feet on the ground. I hope we don't run into *Hauptsturmführer* Bock again. He's a captain in the S.S. and I don't think he will have taken it as a joke. No sense of humour, the S.S."

He went on talking for some time, but Sherwood was too tired to listen and within a few minutes was fast asleep.

CHAPTER FIVE

MONSIEUR LEPIC IS AFRAID

THE NEXT morning Krunjes gave them a couple of bicycles to go into Ostend and meet their Resistance contact. He also gave Sherwood a rucksack and some clothes to replace the ones lost on the trawler. He came to the end of the track to see them off. "Remember," he shouted after them, "if you need help, just come back here, boys."

They waved and pushed on into Ostend.

"If he was doing so well on the black market, I don't understand why he was bothering with fishing," Sherwood said suspiciously. "It seems a poor game for him."

Merridew laughed. "Fishing was the least of his activities," he replied. "He was only using that as a blind for smuggling diesel oil out of the docks. If he could do a job for the Resistance at the same time, so much the better. No, there aren't any flies on Krunjes. He's a good lad really, just a simple pirate at heart."

Already they were in the town mixing with the crowds of cyclists on their way to work. There were scarcely any cars about other than German military vehicles. All the Belgians were either walking or cycling.

Four years of occupation had obviously taken their toll. Everyone looked tired and rather shabby and the shops they passed were mostly empty of goods. It was a depressing picture which even the crisp, sunny morning did nothing to improve.

The address which Krunjes had given to them turned out to be a ship-chandler's shop in a small square near the docks. It was a shabby, two-story building which had seen better days. Faded and peeling letters over the door gave the owner's name as "Lepic." One or two other merchants and seedy cafés made up the square. Obviously they were all being affected by the war and the falling-off of sea-borne trade.

"This is where we spilt up, laddie. There's no point in our both sticking our necks out," said Merridew. "We'll ditch the bicycles in this side-street and go into the square separately. You will go to the café opposite the chandler's shop, sit on the terrace and order a coffee. Keep your eyes skinned. If everything is all right I'll come to the shop door and look out as though expecting someone. Then join me, but not otherwise. If I leave the shop and walk off, let me get clear and then tag along behind, in case I'm being followed. I'll let you know when you can catch me up, but

keep your eyes on me because I may dodge about
a bit to throw any shadows off. All right——?"

Sherwood nodded. That seemed to cover everything.

Merridew's grin reappeared briefly. "Well, give
me a couple of minutes, then follow me into
the square. Chin up, Rule Britannia and so
forth."

Sherwood waited impatiently for a few minutes
after Merridew had disappeared round the corner,
then propped his bike against the wall and followed.

Merridew had already entered the shop, so
Sherwood made his way to the café and sat down
at a table on the terrace. The scruffy-looking
patron came out and flicked the table with a cloth.
"It's warmer inside," he said when Sherwood
ordered a coffee. "We have a fire to-day."

"I prefer the fresh air," replied Sherwood,
trying to sound convincing.

The *patron* shrugged understandingly. "So you
saw them, too. They've been here for a couple of
days now. I don't know what they're waiting for.
It's hard for a patriot, but one has to earn a living."

He shuffled off, leaving Sherwood wondering
what he had been talking about. Then he saw for
himself and his blood ran cold, for out of the
window of the café stared the swarthy face of the

man he had last seen glaring up from the escaping car in Hampstead. The man was in civilian clothes, but behind him there were other figures in the field-grey of German Army uniform.

Sherwood's first impulse was to rush straight across to warn Merridew, but forcing himself to be casual, he put some coins on the table and strolled off the terrace, round the square, glancing at the shops. He stopped outside the ship-chandler's and peered through the window, but the interior was too dark for him to see anything.

Merridew had given strict enough instructions for Sherwood not to follow him into the shop unless he first came to the door. But Sherwood knew that this was an emergency which had not been allowed for. If the swarthy-faced agent had brought photographs of them from Hampstead, then their chances of getting away would, in any case, be pretty slim.

He braced himself and went inside. There was a strong smell of tarred rope and paraffin and, as his eyes became accustomed to the half light, he saw that the shop was stocked to the ceiling with untidy piles of marine stores.

He moved quietly towards the back of the shop and heard someone speaking below. Behind some bales of fishing-nets there was a staircase down to the basement. As he crept towards the stairs there was a slight movement behind him. Spinning round, he found himself looking straight down the muzzle of Merridew's automatic.

"I told you not to come until I gave the signal," Merridew rapped angrily, but his expression quickly changed when he heard what had happened at the café.

"Old Lepic was right, then," he said. "We've not a minute to lose if we're to get clear. I must tell the old boy—he's downstairs telephoning." But before he could go down, a yellow-faced, rather shrunken old man came slowly up into the shop. He stared at Sherwood for a minute without speaking, then seized Merridew's arm; his hand was shaking like a leaf.

"I have spoken to Yves," he said breathlessly. "Naturally I could say little by phone, but he has agreed to meet you. You will be taken to him."

When Merridew told him about the Germans in the café opposite, the old man nearly collapsed. "I am too old for this work," he said bitterly, "but I will take you to the place where you are to wait. We must go by the back way. Hurry, please."

He led the way through the rear of the shop, out to a gate into the yard of the building next door, then into a narrow and evil-smelling passage which wound between derelict stores and stables. They continued along a maze of deserted alleys for about a quarter of an hour, then the old man halted and pointed to a red-bricked building some way ahead.

"There," he said, "that is where you will be met. At the end of this path there is an un-locked door into that warehouse. Go in and wait. You will be fetched. Now I will say good-bye, for I must go back."

"Must you?" said Merridew.

The same thought had occurred to Sherwood. The chances were that the old man would walk straight into the arms of the waiting Germans if he returned to his shop.

"I must," he replied shakily. "There are things I must destroy before the Germans come. Besides, I am too old; I should be a burden to you. Now, it is for the young man. Good luck, boys, and be brave." He embraced them each on both cheeks and hurried away, wiping his eyes, before they could say anything.

"Doesn't it make you mad!" muttered Merridew savagely, "to see an old man like that chivvied around by a lot of thugs!"

He turned abruptly and led the way to the warehouse, which, as Monsieur Lepic had said, was unlocked. Inside, the gloomy building was so full of stored furniture, that it was hardly possible to move about. The furniture was covered with dust-sheets, which gave it a ghostly appearance in the dim light filtering through the grimy glass panels in the roof.

"Comfortable, but not vulgar," said Merridew, quickly recovering his spirits. "Well, I suppose we had better settle down and wait. I've no idea how long we'll have to be here. First of all we'll scout round and see how the land lies in case we have to get out in a hurry."

They examined all the possible exits and decided that, in an emergency, the best escape route would be back the way they had come. If that should be blocked, the next best would be up a cat ladder and out through a hatch on to a furniture hoist projecting over the walled forecourt in front of the warehouse; from there, with luck, they could jump on to the parapet of the next building and make off across the roofs.

They decided, too, to keep watch on the road outside and, as there were no windows near the floor, selected a platform below their escape hatch as a vantage point. If the hatch were left a few inches open, they had a commanding view along the narrow street.

They took turns at this until late in the afternoon, then, while Sherwood was on watch, Merridew came up and squatted beside him. They munched some black bread and sausage which Krunjes had given to them and shared a bottle of lager beer that had, no doubt, been intended for a German mess.

"I'm not too happy about this Resistance group we're contacting," said Merridew. "There are some very efficient ones in Ostend, but this one we don't know much about. I don't like the way the Jerries have been able to watch Lepic's shop for several days without them knowing. They should have taken precautions against that sort of thing."

Sherwood had not thought of that, but the long wait was making him uneasy too.

"Couldn't we make a break for the Ardennes ourselves?" he suggested. "After all, the object of this exercise is to get there and investigate Project 38 as quickly as possible."

Merridew grunted. "Maybe you're right," he agreed, "but we'll get no outside help there. The Jerries have cleaned up the Resistance completely. We need all the information we can get and if this wounded chap can give us an idea of the layout of the installation, it'll have been worth the delay. He should be able to; after all, he's been right in there."

A thought struck Sherwood: "Why haven't we had aerial photographs?" he asked.

"We tried four times, and lost the plane each time. We could have had them in the end, I expect, but we would still have needed an investigation on the ground. No, laddie, I'm afraid we'd better hang around until . . ."

Sherwood waved to him to be quiet for a van, without lights, was cruising slowly along the street towards them.

Merridew knelt behind him and looked over his shoulder.

"It may be our contact. But we won't disclose ourselves—we'll let them come and look for us."

The van crept by the gates of the forecourt and stopped. No one got out, nothing happened. It just stayed there.

After a while Merridew whispered that he would check the alley at the back and disappeared silently down the cat ladder.

A few minutes later the back door slammed and furniture was dragged about on the floor below. Merridew came racing breathlessly back up the ladder. " We've been surrounded," he panted, "and it's not by the Resistance, either. I've blocked the back door for the time being, but we've got to get out at once."

As he spoke a whistle shrilled in the street. The doors of the van burst open and black-uniformed figures sprang out and rushed up to the forecourt gate. At the same time there was a crashing on the back door as someone tried to break it down.

Sherwood shoved open the hatch to climb out on to the hoist. The only chance now was to get on to the neighbouring roof before the Germans were in the forecourt. Once inside, they would straightaway be able to spot anyone on the hoist, which was only thirty feet or so above the ground.

Sherwood had just thrown one leg over the sill when a beam of light blazed up from the warehouse floor and played straight on to him.

A voice, cutting through the darkness, ordered in French:

"Do not resist, or we shall shoot. Come down, both of you, at once!"

CHAPTER SIX

WAR IN A CELLAR

THE BATTERING on the back door continued and the forecourt gates splintered apart, but Merridew and Sherwood still hesitated to move until the order was repeated more urgently.

Merridew shrugged. "We'd better do as they say," he said and slid down the ladder.

They had no sooner reached the floor than they were seized and half-led, half-dragged through the darkness towards the side of the warehouse. As the lamp flashed on again for an instant, it showed a massive wardrobe, swung aside to uncover an open steel door on which it was mounted. The cool air blowing in was like a refreshing shower of cold water, which cleared Sherwood's head of the musty atmosphere of the warehouse. He suddenly realised that they were being rescued, not captured, but when he turned to Merridew, he was shoved hurriedly through the opening and told to keep quiet. The door was swung shut, dragging the wardrobe back into place.

The Germans were making enough row shoot-

ing the locks off the front doors to cover the
escape. It occurred to Sherwood that they were
probably not certain that there was anyone in the
warehouse, and with luck, would miss the
concealed door as he and Merridew had done
earlier.

Their rescuers rapidly led the way along an open
passage between deserted buildings to a wall-
grating, beyond which a flight of stone steps ran
down to a series of inter-connected cellars.

"Hurry! Do not speak," they were ordered, and
urged on by the torch flashing ahead. The beam
swept over strange growths on the streaming
cellar walls and the air was heavy with the smell
of decay. The eeriness of the place was heightened
by the muffled, silent figures escorting them.

Before long the lamp seemed to disappear into
the floor. Someone close behind caught Sherwood's arm and said:

"Steady! There are steps which are slippery and
there is water at the bottom."

The warning was just in time, for almost at
once they reached a flight of worn and slimy
treads and the unmistakable sound of flowing
water came from far below. At the bottom a
stone landing-stage jutted out into the water of
an underground canal.

The man with the torch, who appeared to be the
leader of the party, was standing with one foot

on the gunwale of a small launch. He beckoned impatiently for them to get in. Merridew squeezed down beside Sherwood.

"This is the real underground," he muttered, but at once the torch shone on him.

"Silence!" snapped the leader, "there will be no talking." He swung his torch to check that the party was complete. Satisfied, he snapped his fingers. An electric motor hummed into life and they were under way.

There were only three other Resistance men besides the leader, which Sherwood found a bit surprising, because in the dark there had seemed to be about a dozen of them. Even so, the small boat was packed so tightly that there was no room to move.

It was quite uncanny, sitting there in the darkness with only the quiet whine of the motor and the sloshing of water against the sides of the tunnel breaking the silence. There were occasional gusts of fresh air and glimpses of the starlit sky as they passed along short open stretches, but for the most part they were in tunnel.

Now and again the leader's torch lit up underground landing-stages, showing that this waterway was used for transporting goods and was probably linked with the docks and main canal system covering Belgium and Northern Europe.

Sherwood found it difficult to keep track of time but the journey was long enough for him to be cramped and stiff before it was over.

Eventually the engine was switched off, and they nosed into a jetty where several boats were already tied up. The leader waved everyone out of the launch and up a flight of steps. In all this time the Resistance escort had made no attempt to talk, and, in fact, had maintained the strictest silence.

At the head of the steps was a heavy, timber door reinforced with studs and metal strips like a castle gate. It was opened by two men carrying Sten guns, and the party passed through into a vast cellar with a low, vaulted roof, supported by lines of massive, brick pillars stretching out of sight into the darkness. The bays between the pillars were stacked to the roof with barrels, either side of loading gangways. Above these central ways, on thick timber beams, were overhead tracks carrying gantries. Here and there bare electric bulbs threw a dim light which increased rather than relieved the gloom.

"Cheerful place," murmured Merridew, "looks like the basement of a brewery. I'll have to suggest it to Colonel Nick. He's got no imagination in picking headquarters for us!"

At first glance the place seemed to be deserted, but as the leader turned into a side gangway, a much stronger glow of light was to be seen coming from one of the bays straight ahead. From the outside the walls of barrels appeared part of a solid pile, but inside, a compartment about forty feet by twenty feet had been hollowed out and was in use as the depot and headquarters of the Resistance group. Along one side were stacks of rifles, boxes of grenades and ammunition; along another, bunks and bedding, and against a third, wireless equipment and a large map-board. But it was the table, with five men seated round it, which immediately caught Sherwood's attention.

The reception committee watched silently as he and Merridew approached. It was not an enthusiastic welcome by any means. The man at the head got up and stalked towards them. He was a tough specimen with battered features and small eyes. He inspected them silently.

"I wish to see Yves," said Merridew shortly. "I have a message for him."

"I am Yves," replied the Resistance chief. "What is your message?"

"The message is, 'The chickens come home to roost'."

The chief continued his examination until it became offensive.

"You've heard about us from London," went on Merridew with mounting irritation. "You have been instructed to put us in touch with Latour from Dinant. Does that satisfy you?"

"No," said Yves, "it does not satisfy me because I know that you are German agents."

That completely took the wind out of Sherwood's sails. He stared at Yves stupidly and even Merridew seemed at a loss for words.

"We are not complete fools and we still have our informants," continued Yves, obviously pleased with the effect of his accusation. "We know what happened when Krunjes's boat landed. We know he was arrested and there were no Englishmen with him; but you two were seen entering the police van—of your own free will . . ." He held up his hand as Merridew tried to interrupt. "That is not all, Boche! You were seen entering old Lepic's shop and an hour later it was raided by the S.S. and he was arrested. You managed to arrange the rendezvous at the warehouse and, sure enough, that, too, was raided, but this time we were expecting it. You did not know this, but you were under observation from the moment you entered the warehouse. My men waited until the raid before disclosing themselves because we wanted to be sure. You were hoping to trap my men as well, weren't you, Boche?" He fairly spat the word out. "Well, it is you who are trapped and you will be shot later to-night, but first we want information. You can give it to us willingly, or we will extract it from you—it is up to you! Personally I hope we have to extract it!" He blinked cunningly as he let this sink in.

Sherwood's first thought was to make a jump for one of the Sten guns, but before he could move Merridew spoke up. He was blazing with anger:

"You stupid, incompetent fool!" he hissed at Yves, "you're not fit to be in charge of a nursery, let alone a Resistance group. It is due to blundering, clod-hopping, heavy-fisted, dull-witted, self-important fools like you that the Germans ever entered your country at all! It's due to people like you that the Germans have been rolling up your Resistance like an old carpet.

"You've seen Project 38—you helped smuggle it to England—but you're too busy knocking off an odd German here and there to realise that you had the biggest thing in the war in your hands. I've brought this man, an artillery expert, to risk his neck in the Ardennes doing your job for you, and all you can do is to cook up an absurd story like this!"

If the tough-looking Resistance types were shaken by this outburst, so was Sherwood. He thought Merridew would get them both shot on the spot, but Merridew had not finished.

"I've been parachuted three times into France and twice into Belgium," he went on, "but I've never seen such a wrap-up as this. When London hears of this you won't get another farthing, nor another round of ammunition—they'll avoid you like the plague."

The surprise on Yves's face would have been comical in other circumstances. "This is very well," he blustered, "but what about Krunjes and Lepic? You do not answer these charges."

"Charges!" echoed Merridew scornfully. "The only charges are of your inefficiency. Where is Krunjes? In which prison? Do you know that?— Of course you don't, because at this minute he's sitting in his black-market depot outside Ostend, where we spent the night with him. As for Lepic, you saw us enter his shop, but did you know that the Germans had been watching him from a café opposite for the last two days? The *patron* would have told you, if you had bothered to ask. You should be ashamed to have left an old man like Lepic in a key position while you were playing cops and robbers in and out of tunnels and cellars."

Yves hesitated and looked to his companions as though inviting their opinion. One of them leaned across the table and whispered to him. His face cleared and he nodded. The other man came and stood by Sherwood.

"You say you are an English soldier?" asked Yves.

Sherwood told him that he was and gave his name, rank and regimental number.

"You speak good French," Yves said suspiciously and shrugged his shoulders.

At this signal, the man standing by Sherwood swung round and slapped him full force across the face. Sherwood felt that his head had been nearly knocked right off; it rang like a peal of bells and the half-healed cuts from the explosion at Larkhill burned like fire. He leaped for his assailant, but two other men grabbed him, so he gave the company the benefit of his best barrack-room adjectives. Most of them came from a drill sergeant at Woolwich, an old sweat with thirty years' service, and the largest vocabulary on record. It was an impressive performance.

Yves listened in silence, and when Sherwood had finally run out of steam, shrugged his shoulders again.

"This man is an English soldier—I can vouch for it," he said to his companions. Then he added simply: "My apologies, Messieurs. I was mistaken."

He seemed to think that that made everything all right, but Merridew was not so easily satisfied.

"Well, if you have finished knocking my friend about," he said sarcastically, "perhaps we can get on with the job we're here for. I want to know where Latour is—can you tell me or do you want to play other games first!"

Yves glared at him resentfully.

"Because if you do," continued Merridew mercilessly, "you had better see if I'm armed, hadn't you?" His automatic appeared in his hand, aimed directly at the Resistance chief's throat. "You really are not very good, are you?"

Yves was beaten, and he knew it. He sat down heavily as Merridew's automatic vanished again.

"It is easy to criticise. We try our best," he said.

"Well done," insisted Merridew relentlessly. "If you will now tell us where Latour is, we will get out of here and leave you to go on trying."

"He is in the sanatorium at De Haan about five kilometres east of Ostend."

Merridew stared at him incredulously. "But that is a German military hospital—how could he be there?"

"It was my idea," replied Yves, his spirits reviving a bit. "When he came to us he was seriously ill. He had been badly wounded escaping from the Ardennes and still had three bullets in him which needed removing quickly. It could only be done in a hospital. We took him to De Haan and made out that he was a collaborator who had been shot up by patriots. It was a good idea," he added defiantly.

"I suppose the Germans would not be suspicious when they dug German bullets out of your unfortunate friend?" asked Merridew scathingly.

Yves flushed angrily and was about to reply, when the silence outside the compartment was broken by the sound of someone running along the gallery towards them, shouting wildly. The voice was muffled by the barrel walls, but it sounded so panic-stricken that all the Resistance men leapt to their feet, grabbing for their Stens.

A man Sherwood had not seen before burst in. "The Germans!" he shouted. "There are truck-loads of them! They're in the yard. The lads up there won't be able to hold them!"

As if to confirm what he said, a burst of auto-matic firing echoed faintly through the cellar. It was followed in rapid succession by others, until the din became continuous.

Yves looked about him desperately. "We must abandon this place. Pick up as much as you can and get down to the boats," he shouted, seizing several rifles.

Merridew grabbed his arm. "Never mind the rifles," he snapped. "Save the wireless and the explosives."

Yves, who had evidently forgotten about Merridew and Sherwood in the emergency, swung round triumphantly.

"You *are* Boche spies," he shouted. All his resentment at the tongue-lashing Merridew had given him, boiled up. "You have betrayed us, too! But this is the last time!" He dropped the rifles and grabbed his Sten. At the same time there was a crash at the far end of the cellar, followed by a blast of firing. The air was filled with bullets striking sparks from the stone flags and thudding into the massive barrels.

Merridew and Sherwood moved at the same instant. Merridew leapt back, kicking at the chocks holding the barrels in place, while Sherwood dived at Yves's legs.

The Sten flared. There was a stunning shock in Sherwood's left arm as he made contact and bowled Yves over. Then the lights went out, plunging them into darkness and complete chaos. Above the ear-splitting racket of the sub-machine guns, there was a rumbling as the wall of barrels started to collapse. It moved slowly at first, then with increasing speed until, for a few moments, the cellar was filled with thunder.

Sherwood dragged himself up to find Merridew shining a torch he had grabbed on to some up-ended barrels standing by a brick pillar.

"Up there, Sherwood," he yelled, swinging his rucksack over his shoulder.

They clambered up until they were clear of the floor. Merridew pointed to the track of the gantry over their heads and swung himself up-wards.

Sherwood tried to follow, but found his left arm was useless. Merridew leaned back and hauled him up until he managed to get one leg over a rail and lever himself up on to the track. Like that they were sheltered from below by the steel sections, and the only immediate danger was from the ricochets screaming wildly from the vaulted roof just above their heads.

"Keep down!" said Merridew, "I'll have a look at your arm."

The battle beneath was still raging furiously and the air was full of cries and groans as bullets found their mark. From the position of the torch flashes it looked as though the survivors of the Resistance group were succeeding in falling back to the steps down to the canal.

"It's a flesh wound," said Merridew, "have to see about it later. Hang on here while I see where the track leads." He crawled away, leaving Sherwood with his rucksack. Before he went, he knocked out two light bulbs hanging nearby—"Just in case the electricity comes on again," he said.

It was just as well he did, for a few moments after he disappeared the firing stopped. There were one or two shots over by the steps, then it was finished. Apparently some of the Resistance had got away in their boats.

Sherwood had just finished stuffing a handkerchief up his sleeve to stop the blood running down over his hand when the lights came on again. Thanks to Merridew's foresight, the gantry track was in deep shadow. German troops poured into the cellar and started a systematic search. It did not take them long to uncover the cache of arms and equipment and one of them hurried off to report the find. He returned quickly with several officers. As they came into the brighter light of the compartment Sherwood froze, for there were two he recognised. The first was Captain Bock—but it was the second that took his attention, for it was the swarthy man from Hampstead, now dressed in the field-grey of the German Army, whom he had last seen staring out of the café window at the shop of Monsieur Lepic.

CHAPTER SEVEN

MERRIDEW CHANGES CLOTHES

THE SWARTHY man sat down, mopping his face and watching impassively while Bock rooted excitedly through the captured equipment.

"Well, Colonel Schieffen," said Bock, oozing self-satisfaction, "you have seen for yourself how the S.S. works. Perhaps you understand now why we think that we should be in charge of military intelligence instead of the *Abwehr*."

The officer he addressed moved out of the shadows without replying. He was tall and thin, straight as a ramrod, with a white face so expressionless that it was like a mask. He, also, was in field-grey. He inspected the captured arms and equipment slowly and carefully.

"I congratulate you, Captain Bock," he said in a dry, cold voice, "you have captured—let me see —twelve British rifles; four Sten guns, two of which are damaged; six boxes of ammunition which appear to be for anti-tank rifles; an obsolete French wireless transmitter, and—ah, yes— four wooden bunks and about a dozen unclean blankets. Well done! Most useful! I am sure that such valuable equipment is what the German Army needs—well worth the three of your men reported killed and the six wounded. The Führer will be pleased with you!"

Bock flushed. "The Colonel does not understand," he retorted. "We have just wiped out the most dangerous Resistance gang which was threatening the Occupation Forces in Ostend."

The Colonel looked about him as though searching for someone. "I accept your word for this, Captain Bock, although I see no evidence. There appear to be only two prisoners, whom you will no doubt torture to death, as you did the unfortunate Lepic earlier this evening, in order to get this address. Yet the Resistance leader seems to have got away, and there is no sign of the two Englishmen you are reported to have helped ashore. But still, no doubt you have blocked the exits from the tunnel and will bring them in later."

It was clear from Bock's embarrassed expression that he had taken no such precaution. He decided to counter-attack, to cover his confusion.

"If Delacroix here," he pointed at the swarthy man, "had not so carelessly destroyed the photographs of the British agents, we should now have them safely under lock and key, Colonel."

Colonel Schieffen laughed unpleasantly and moved off towards the canal steps. Bock followed, explaining and arguing, but not making much impression. The man called Delacroix remained behind. He watched the S.S. carting away the captured equipment, his thick features expression-less. Sherwood had a good chance of observing him as he lolled against an up-ended barrel. Although he was squat and fat, there was a wary alertness about him that suggested he would be a dangerous man to be up against, far more danger-ous than the brutal Bock could ever hope to be.

His dark, heavily pouched eyes flickered to and fro, taking everything in, missing nothing—or so Sherwood thought. Directly he was alone, he bent down to examine the floor closely. Frowning, he straightened up and slowly waddled across the compartment towards the pile of barrels. Sher-wood realised suddenly that Delacroix was follow-ing the trail of blood from his arm, that it must lead up across the barrels and point to his hiding-place.

At that moment Delacroix looked up. To Sher-wood it seemed the dark eyes were staring straight into his face. He froze, waiting to be challenged; but, a second later, Delacroix turned away. Sherwood could hardly believe that he had not been spotted and put it down to the light shining in Delacroix's eyes. Whatever the reason, the narrowness of his escape left him shaken to the core.

As Delacroix turned away he shrugged and casually pushed one of the lower barrels with his foot. It rolled across the floor, wiping out the trail of blood. A neat jet of beer squirted on to the floor from a bullet-hole in the cask.

"Help me set this up," he chuckled to the S.S. men who were returning for more equipment, "then drinks will be on the house."

They stood the barrel up and produced some mugs from the captured stores. The rest of the squad quickly gathered round. Delacroix smiled sardonically to himself before strolling off to meet Colonel Schieffen and Captain Bock, who were returning from inspecting the landing-stage.

Bock shouted angrily when he saw his men slacking, and they hastily got on with their job of dismantling the Resistance headquarters.

"Project 38 is a military operation, Bock," the Colonel was saying as they re-entered the compartment. "The *Abwehr* will be responsible for its security, until the Führer orders otherwise. You will co-operate with me and inform me of anything you do directly affecting it. Is that clear? Now tell me—what is your next move? That is, if you have thought so far ahead."

Bock was furiously angry, but dared not show it too openly to the Colonel. His flabby, white features trembled with his efforts to control himself. "I shall fetch Latour from hospital to-night," he spluttered. "I shall confront him with the two prisoners we've taken. He thinks he's fooled us about being a collaborator, but with what Lepic told us and what these two will tell us, we'll get the truth out of him about the Resistance in the Ardennes by to-morrow morning."

"When you have, report to me," snapped the Colonel and, turning on his heel, stalked off, with Delacroix at his heels.

Bock drew himself up, glaring balefully, and gave the Nazi salute. "Heil Hitler," he bawled, but the Colonel ignored him and kept straight on.

Bock was standing just beneath Sherwood and for the moment there was no one near him. Sherwood thought of what the Colonel had said about Monsieur Lepic dying under Bock's questioning, and groped for his automatic . . . just one shot at point-blank range—it would have been too easy!

But before he could reach it, Merridew re-appeared and signalled him to follow. They crawled the whole length of the cellar along the track. It was heavy going for Sherwood as the numbness was wearing off and sharp twinges were shooting up his arm.

There was a goods lift at the end, with a closed shaft running right up through the building. As the gantry led directly to the lift, it was not difficult to get to a vertical inspection ladder inside the shaft, without being spotted.

"So far, so good," breathed Merridew. "We'd better not try to get out on the ground floor, there'll be too many Jerries about."

He was right. As they climbed past ground-floor level they could hear the Germans ransacking the place.

The first floor was silent and in darkness but the gates could not be opened from the inside. They just would not budge and Merridew dared not make too much noise trying to force them.

"It's no use, laddie," he panted. "We'll have to go up to the second floor. Can you make it, do you think?"

Sherwood nodded, not feeling as confident as he tried to appear. It is practically impossible to climb a vertical ladder using only one hand, and that was what it was boiling down to as his left arm was almost useless. However, they had only gone up a few more rungs when they found an inspection door in the side of the shaft. It gave on to a catwalk running along a glass canopy which projected from the side of the brewery over the front yard.

There was a fair amount of activity below, where the S.S. lorries were being loaded.

"I can't see where it leads to," whispered Merridew, "but we'd better keep moving and get as far from the cellar as possible. We'll be hidden from the yard, at any rate."

They went on hands and knees again and reached the corner of the brewery without incident. The canopy continued along a second side, which was in darkness. A few yards farther on Merridew stopped abruptly and pointed. Over by the boundary wall was a Volkswagen with the driver in S.S. uniform leaning against it, minding his own business and having a quiet smoke. It was a tricky moment. The driver obviously had not seen them, but they would have had to cross his line of sight if they had gone on. Even in the bad light he was bound to notice the movement. They would probably have had to stay still until he had moved off, but a door under the canopy opened and someone called across and distracted him.

"You needn't hang around, Stieger—the Captain's taking a truck out to De Haan. He won't want you again to-night, so get off back to the barracks."

The driver waved an acknowledgment, but did not hurry himself.

"Wait here," hissed Merridew. "Don't move until I call you," and crept away into the shadows.

For a few moments nothing happened. The only sound came from the lorries revving up near the main gate. Something seemed to move near the boundary wall, but when Sherwood looked again there was nothing stirring. Then the glowing cigarette end shot up straight into the air and the driver disappeared with a heavy thud. Merridew appeared round the side of the car and waved.

"Go to the end of the catwalk," he called softly. "There's a ladder there."

Two minutes later Sherwood joined him by the Volkswagen.

"Have you got my rucksack? Good! Get in. I'll be right back," said Merridew, and dragged the unconscious driver away into the darkness.

When he reappeared he was dressed in the driver's greatcoat and cap. "If this is Bock's car, laddie, we shouldn't have any trouble. Just duck down out of sight until we are through the gates. I'll let you know when you can surface again." He shouted something to the sentry posted at the main gate. The man laughed and shouted back, and they were through into the street. It was as easy as that!

All the same, Sherwood's troubles were not over until they stopped in a side road and he was able to uncoil. However good Volkswagens may be, they are a bit cramped if you want to crouch on the floor behind the driver, and his arm was becoming too painful to touch.

Merridew listened silently while Sherwood told

him about the conversation between Bock and Colonel Schieffen.

"There's nothing else for it," he decided when Sherwood had finished, "we'll have to go straight on to De Haan and see if we can get to Latour first. If Bock gets at him now, our job in the Ardennes will be twice as difficult. Maybe we can have your arm attended to at the same time."

The roads were fairly clear of traffic and the S.S. signs on the car and Merridew's black uniform ensured that they were not held up. They were soon clear of Ostend and heading eastwards.

CHAPTER EIGHT

RESCUE OF AN INVALID

As THEY SPED along the coast road behind the sand-dunes, the defences of the West Wall loomed up out of the darkness. The Germans had fortified the whole Belgian and French north coasts against the threat of Allied invasion, and the massive pill-boxes and gun emplacements showed all too clearly what a tough job lay ahead before Germany could be defeated.

Their dimmed headlights picked out signs on both sides of the road with "*Achtung Minen*" and the skull and cross-bones painted on them, denoting minefields.

Sherwood was thinking rather ruefully about the holidays spent along there with his family before the war, when Merridew broke the silence.

"You know, that business between Schieffen and Bock is the first break we've had. We must make the most of it."

Sherwood had not understood the quarrel between the two Germans and asked what he meant.

"The Nazis and the regular German Army don't get on too well together," he explained. "The

Nazis, as a political party, are jealous of the traditions and reputation of the Army, and the Regular soldiers rather despise the Nazis as amateurs in uniform."

"That's all very well," said Sherwood bitterly. "They seem to get on well enough when it comes to attacking other countries."

"Well, you know what soldiers are," Merridew went on tactlessly. "Mostly they do what they're told, especially when they're winning. The average German soldier is a decent enough chap, but the Nazis are a different kettle of fish. They've been trained as thugs and they're as vicious as rattlesnakes. There's literally nothing they won't do—you can't trust them an inch. The Army's secret service, which is called the *Abwehr*, is responsible for all military intelligence work. The S.S. have their own intelligence service, too, under a chap called Schellenberg, and they're trying to muscle in on the military side of things. Himmler, the S.S. Chief, is very close to Hitler, while Canaris, the *Abwehr* king-pin, is losing favour. So you see it's all a bit tricky."

"How does that affect us? They're both out to catch us, aren't they?"

"Never doubt it, laddie. But my guess is that the Project 38 installation is guarded by the *Abwehr* and the S.S. are trying to nose their way in. At the moment I don't know how we can use it, but just keep it in mind. Look——" Merridew broke off, "——you'd better watch out for direction signs to the hospital. We can't be far off De Haan now."

They slowed down and Sherwood stuck his head out of the window. In the blackout it was difficult to pick out directions, but after another kilometre or so there was a large Red Cross sign.

"Right," said Merridew. "Now don't forget you're 'Michel Richard.' You're a Belgian electrical engineer working for the Todt Labour Organisation, and you've been shot accidentally. While your arm is being attended to I'll snoop around and try to locate Latour."

It was a bit like going into the lion's den, but everything was very quiet as they parked the car behind some shrubs and went up the steps into the hospital.

A duty orderly in the hall directed them to the Casualty Department. Business could not have been brisk, for the place was deserted, and it was some time before they could find anyone to deal with them. Then a sleepy medical sergeant came to look at Sherwood's arm. One glance at Merridew's S.S. uniform satisfied him about them. He did not bother with any questions, but just prepared an anti-tetanus injection and a dressing in a bored, half-hearted sort of way.

"Don't often see the S.S. about here," he said to

Merridew. "Then we have two visits in one evening. Are we going to have a purge or something? You can shoot our Major if you like, and while you're about it, you can knock off the Adjutant, too! Do us all a favour!"

"Two visits?" queried Merridew. "Has our Captain Bock been here?"

"Captain Something-or-other," said the sergeant. "Nasty-looking piece of work—shouting about the place as though he owned it. Came to fetch a Belgian chap. Still here, I think, having a row with the Adjutant. Prize couple they make."

Merridew nodded and disappeared, while the sergeant rather untidily finished off the bandaging.

"There you are, son," he yawned, "compliments of the Führer!"

Sherwood muttered his thanks and hurried back to find Merridew waiting outside.

"I think Bock is still here," said Merridew. "There's an S.S. truck and driver round the corner. Now this is what we're going to do. We can't create a row here, so I'm going to relieve Bock's driver quietly. You follow the truck in the car, and when we're on a quiet stretch of road, I'll deal with Bock, then we'll transfer Latour to the car and make a break for Krunjes's hide-out. We'll just have to hope that Lepic knew nothing about it, otherwise he might have given it away when Bock questioned him. Do you think you can manage to drive with your arm like that?"

Sherwood reassured him, but thought it seemed a pretty risky scheme. However, as with most risky schemes it worked like a charm.

When Bock appeared, he was too busy with his prisoner to notice the change of drivers which Merridew had effected noiselessly if not painlessly.

Four or five kilometres down the road the truck pulled in to the side and when Sherwood went up to see if any help was wanted, Bock was already out cold with a trickle of blood running down from his temple while Merridew was reluctantly tucking away his automatic.

"I ought to shoot him," he said regretfully, "for what he did to old Lepic and no doubt many others, but in cold blood, I just can't do it."

He helped a heavily-bandaged figure from the back of the truck and led him to the car. As an afterthought, Sherwood let the air out of the truck tyres in case Bock recovered too quickly.

"You're learning, laddie," chuckled Merridew when he saw what Sherwood was doing. "Hop in—I'll drive."

This time he avoided Ostend and skirted round the built-up area. He obviously had an eye for country even in the dark because he did not hesitate once. Even so, it was not a quick journey and the sky was beginning to pale in the east as they arrived at the entrance to the lane, leading to Krunjes's hide-out.

They narrowly escaped being riddled with bullets by the lookout, who must have had the shock of his life, to see a car with S.S. markings suddenly appear. He continued to be suspicious until Krunjes himself turned up and welcomed them like long-lost brothers. Latour, who had been silent throughout the journey, seemed dazed and too exhausted by the rapid turn of events to talk. Merridew told him to turn-in and get some sleep first. After they had seen him safely bedded down, they joined Krunjes in the farm-house.

He did not seem surprised at the break-up of the Resistance group, and was openly contemptuous of their organisation.

"This is why I do not join them," he said, shaking his head. "I do jobs for them, but join them—no! I should have warned you. They put all their eggs in one box. Now they lose everything—wireless, guns, ammunition, and if the Boches have blocked the canal . . ." He drew a finger across his throat.

He grunted approval over the rescue of Latour. "The Boches will not take this lying down," he said thoughtfully. "They will search the country-side and they will find this place. We must go."

"Sorry if we're bringing you trouble, Krunjes," said Merridew. "You've been a good friend."

Krunjes brushed the apology aside and beamed. "It is nothing. We are always ready to move. I have much money. I will go and spend it in Switzerland. First to Brussels, then to Switzerland. It is prepared."

Merridew looked at him shrewdly. "How will you go to Switzerland?"

"Through the south of Belgium to France," grinned Krunjes, "then to Switzerland. I used to have a smuggling business with France and Switzerland, before the war. Easy!"

Merridew was silent for a moment. "Look," he said at length, "we have to get into the Ardennes. We can't expect any help from what is left of the Resistance after what's happened. They'll probably be gunning for us, like the Jerries. Will you help us if you're going through the south of Belgium?"

Krunjes's bushy eyebrows shot up. "Help you?" he echoed. "When you risk yourselves to get me away from the Boches? You're my friends, eh? Of course I help you! What you want me to do?"

He shook hands with them both to show his good faith.

"You're a good scout," grinned Merridew. "I can't be sure what we'll need until I've had a chat with Latour. First of all, though, we'll have to go to Brussels because I've a radio operator contact there who'll send some messages to London. That's important. Also I'll have to get Latour to Charleroi, where he can rest up safely before getting out of the country. After that, how we tackle the Ardennes depends on what Latour tells us."

Krunjes nodded several times.

"Good! Good!" he rumbled. "I also go to Brussels. I have friends who will let me have a barge there, and we can go south by canal. I know the canals a long time," he winked at Sherwood who thought to himself that no doubt the police would have been glad to find out some of the things Krunjes knew about the canals. "My friends will take this Latour to Charleroi. It is not far from Brussels, eh? Good!"

He told them his plans. He would start off in a few hours by road, carting a load of "potatoes" to the capital as a cover. Merridew suggested that only Latour should go with Krunjes and that he and Sherwood should go separately by train. A party of four carting one load of potatoes would have looked a bit suspicious, and in any case there would be hardly enough room in the lorry.

The forged papers provided for Sherwood by Major Burke included a curfew pass, an undated permit for travel between Ostend and Charleroi, a journey which, in any case, involved a change of trains in Brussels. Merridew had thoughtfully provided himself with travel-permits for pretty well everywhere in Belgium, where they were necessary, and so was not worried by the prospect of travelling by train, either.

It only remained to get what information they could from Latour about the Project 38 installation in the Ardennes. This they did, after a meal and a short rest.

Latour was a middle-aged, rather sickly man, who had been a booking-clerk on the railways. He was still weak from his wounds, and in a state of shock which made him confused and rather vague about the details of what he had seen.

He soon made it clear, however, that they could expect no help locally in the Ardennes. The area had been thoroughly combed by the *Abwehr* and the S.S., and not only had the local Resistance movement been smashed, but also anyone likely to give trouble had been deported, and that meant pretty well every able-bodied person.

The weapon he had smuggled out had been taken during a raid on some experimental sheds near Dinant. That raid had been the last despairing attempt by the local Resistance before they were broken up.

He produced a very rough sketch of the installation layout, but admitted that much of it was guess-work. It showed jetties on the River Meuse for the landing of water-borne equipment which was stored in depots near Dinant. He said that large numbers of giant earth-shifting machines had been brought in, which suggested that the Germans were burrowing underground. This had been confirmed by the identification of Army mining units arriving by rail. There was a large camp for forced labour containing thousands of prisoners-of-war who were guarded by German troops. The surrounding forests were so thickly mined as to be virtually impenetrable.

The centre of the sketch was taken up by a blank area of which Latour could tell them nothing more than he had seen from a distance through glasses. He said there was a small isolated hill, cleared of trees, from which dozens of vertical ventilating shafts projected a few feet into the air.

"It sounds like an underground factory," suggested Sherwood.

Latour agreed that it could be, and added that many German civilian technicians were known to be living and working in this inner zone.

"Maybe you're right," said Merridew doubtfully, "but isn't it odd for an obviously important factory to be built in Belgium, rather than Germany itself where security and transport would be easier?"

Latour shrugged. From then on it seemed largely guess-work, but one immediately important fact emerged: the best chance of getting into the area was from the River Meuse, where the new jetties were; Latour said that barges were continually arriving and being unloaded by the prisoners-of-war. That fitted in well with Krunjes's plan to travel by water. The only alternative appeared to be the railways, but as they ran through the minefields and were closely guarded, they were not promising.

They thanked Latour for his efforts. He was obviously still in pain and it is impressive to think that, but for the courage of that little grey-faced man, Project 38 might never have been heard of—at least, not until Britain had been brought to her knees.

Shortly after they had finished, Krunjes came in to fetch him; it was time to start.

"Don't forget," he yelled to them above the racket of his "potato" lorry, "I see you at . . . to-morrow night . . . the greengrocer . . ."

The rest of what he shouted was lost as the lorry jolted down the track, but it did not matter, they were hardly likely to forget the place where they were to meet him.

CHAPTER NINE

ROCKETS AND FOUNTAIN-PENS

MERRIDEW DECIDED that a night train would be best because there would be fewer people about and the Gestapo, as the S.S. Police were called, who usually kept an eye on the stations and travellers, would be less alert.

There were two ways of looking at it, and Sherwood thought that if things went wrong, it would be better to go when there were crowds they could lose themselves in.

"It doesn't matter how many people there are about, passengers have to go through the barriers more or less one at a time," reasoned Merridew. "If the Jerries feel interested they'll pick you out. They like playing to the gallery and often make an example of someone in public, just as a warning to everyone else."

Ostend Station was almost deserted when they arrived. There were three Gestapo men on duty, but they were standing in a corner talking and did not even bother inspecting the curfew passes of the few miserable passengers waiting for the Brussels train.

The only precaution Merridew took was to stow his rucksack behind a seat some way from where they waited, and not fetch it until just before the train arrived. As well as the explosive pencils and rulers he had brought from England, he had stuffed in the S.S. uniform he had "borrowed" from Bock's driver.

"It might come in useful," he said cheerfully. "In any case you can only be shot once," which was quite true. If the explosives were discovered on him, the uniform could not make things any worse.

The train was an "omnibus," which meant that it stopped at every station and once or twice in between, just for luck.

They had a compartment to themselves and, in spite of the wooden seats and his arm, which was aching still, Sherwood dozed off as they trundled through the night. In fact, after they had passed through Ghent he went fast asleep and would probably have slept all the way if Merridew had not woken him.

They were on the outskirts of Brussels, stopped beside a marshalling-yard.

"Look over there by the sheds," rapped Merridew.

When Sherwood saw what he was pointing at, it certainly cleared the sleep out of his head. In spite of the blackout, the yard lights were blazing.

Beneath them stood a freight train of open wagons. On each wagon was a single long low crate. On the side of each crate were stencilled the words "Projekt 38." Here, for the first time, was something that Sherwood knew was his business rather than Merridew's. Up until now Merridew had taken all the decisions and Sherwood had followed along, but now it was up to him, and he did not intend to miss the chance.

"I'm going over to get a closer look," he said firmly. "You stay here with the luggage. If this train starts off before I'm back, I'll meet you at the rendezvous with Krunjes."

"Fair enough, laddie," agreed Merridew with a faint grin, showing that he had guessed the way Sherwood was thinking, "but get out on the other side, away from the lights."

Everything was silent except for the slight hiss of escaping steam as Sherwood slipped down on to the track. His boots crunching on the cinders sounded loud enough to wake the yard, but the expected challenge did not come.

The freight train stretched through the yard out into the darkness at either end. He decided to try a wagon on the edge of the lighted area. There would be less risk of being seen there, and a better chance of getting away into the darkness if he were. He picked a likely wagon, keeping well into the shadows, and pulled himself up on the platform. The crate was about five feet square in section and thirty feet long. A closer examination showed that whilst the long sides were made of stout timbers and were reinforced for mechanical handling, the ends were comparatively flimsy and were probably intended only as protection against the weather.

What was needed was a good sheath-knife to prise the end panel loose, but the best thing he had with him was a five-franc piece. It worked the panel out sufficiently for him to squeeze in a finger and widen the gap enough to use the barrel of his automatic as a lever. He strained on the butt until the panel gave with a resounding crack, split in two, one half clattering down on to the track.

This time he was certain the alarm would be given, but then, as if the noise had been the signal, the Ostend train gave a lurch and clattered off on its final stretch into the centre of Brussels. His relief at this diversion was pretty mixed, because the train was taking Merridew with it, leaving him to complete the job alone. However, there was no time to worry about that, and he yanked away the rest of the end panel and peered into the crate. There, stretching away into the dark interior, was a great cylinder with a yellow tapering end towards him. Running down to the point was a white painted letter "V."

He had not known what to expect, but the silent menace of the sleek shape set him back. The glaring white "V" could stand for only one thing—*Vergeltung*—Vengeance, the name the Germans were giving to all their secret weapons.

Then it dawned on him. What he was looking at was a giant version of the weapon he had last seen at Larkhill. That must have been a model, and this was the real Project 38.

There was only one way to be certain and that was to check the other end and see whether it was fitted with retractable fins. He ducked along the wagon and started working on the other end panel of the crate. The noise of the Ostend train had died away and he had to work silently again.

The second panel was even tougher than the first, and he lashed himself up into a fine lather for fear the freight train would start off before he had finished. Finally the panel gave and this one did not split, it came away with only a slight creaking noise. There was no light at this end so he leaned inside and felt around the metal base. Something jabbed into his back.

"Don't move, you Belgian dog!" rasped a voice behind him. "Now—put your hands on your head; turn round and jump to the ground."

When he turned he was confronted by the steel-helmeted figure of a German soldier covering him with his rifle.

"Did you think the train would not be guarded?" asked the guard mockingly. "Come on—jump!" He picked up the automatic from the platform of the wagon and motioned Sherwood to march on ahead down the train. He kept a pace or two behind so that there was no chance for Sherwood to turn on him and deflect his rifle. Obviously he knew his unarmed combat.

"Just my luck," thought Sherwood bitterly, knowing very well that it had been his own fault to be captured at the moment he had literally laid hands on the first important clue to Project 38. For in the few seconds before the guard had appeared, his fingers had been running along the edge of the tell-tale fins, which had been fully retracted into the body of the projectile.

He edged off towards the shadows, but a harsh warning from behind showed that the guard was too experienced to fall for such a feeble trick. As they trudged along Sherwood saw for the first time that every fifth or sixth wagon had an observation cabin which gave a clear view along the train, and kicked himself for not remembering that these were common enough on the Continent.

"Turn off here," growled the sentry. "Head towards the offices."

Once away from the track, there was no hope of escape because the yard was fully lighted. A group of Belgian railway workers watched silently as they passed, and Sherwood had the wild idea of appealing to them for help, but it would have been useless. Even if they had been willing they were unarmed and no match for the Germans.

"Now turn left at the next corner and into the door in front of you."

One last glance round showed no chance of making a last-minute break. Sherwood turned the corner and cannoned head-on into a black-uniformed figure hurrying the other way.

"Bravo!" said a familiar voice. "At last the Army has noticed what is going on under its nose!"

Merridew, who should by this time have been arriving at the Midi Station in the city, straightened his borrowed S.S. cap and thrust his face into Sherwood's.

"Miserable saboteur," he hissed, "I shall teach you to keep your hands off the property of the Reich. I shall deal with this myself. Come with me!"

If Sherwood was staggered by Merridew's sudden appearance, the sentry was put out too, but for a different reason.

"This man is my prisoner," he growled. "I am taking him to the guard-room."

Merridew brandished two rucksacks in the

sentry's face. "You can count, can't you?" he demanded. "There are at least two saboteurs and your sector of the train is now unguarded. Get back to your post—I will take charge of the prisoner and tell the guard commander to relieve you so that you can make your report."

The man hesitated, and Sherwood dared not look at him for fear of giving the game away. The sentry was a good soldier but, like many other good soldiers, his first instinct was to do as he was told and, like many other Germans, he did not want to tangle with the S.S. He grunted and half turned away; then he remembered something and produced Sherwood's automatic.

"The prisoner had this with him. Give it to the guard commander."

Sherwood was in a fury to be off, but Merridew was in no hurry. "Do I have to guess your name?" he barked. "How will the guard commander know who to relieve?"

"Private Bronowski," grumbled the sentry. "I won't be relieved, though, you'll see. I've been on this perishing train without a break since Essen." He made off, pretty disgruntled.

"That's a good German name," called Merridew after him. "Perhaps the Gestapo should investigate you, too!" Then he looked at Sherwood and grinned. "Surprised to see me? You didn't think I'd let you go racketing off by yourself, did

you? Come on, we'll make our way down the
line until we're clear of the yard—and don't
forget, if we're challenged, I've just caught
you."

They wasted no time getting away from the
brilliantly-lit area, following parallel to the railway track. They had not gone far before the open
wagons gave way to tankers carrying liquid in
bulk. In the faint light from the yard, Sherwood
could see that they were painted in the same
bright yellow as the nose of the projectile.

He told Merridew about it, but they decided not
to risk a closer examination.

"There will be observation cabs all along the
train," said Merridew. "This makes it all the more
important to find our radio operator here in
Brussels and get a message back to London."

There are few more tricky operations than walking along a railway track in the dark and, once
clear of the train, this they had to do as there were
ditches either side of the line. It was some time
before they got used to the spacing of the sleepers
and made much headway.

Twice there were air-raid warnings from the
city, but no attack developed and they were more
concerned about being run down by a train than
about being bombed. But no train came, either.
Even so, they were relieved enough to reach a
level-crossing and to leave the railway behind.

"I'd better literally ditch this uniform," said Merridew. "It's too much of a mess to use again."

True enough, the trip along the railway track had not done it much good and it would not have passed muster in daylight.

"Ah, well," he said, bundling it out of sight in the ditch. "I can always get another, I suppose. Matter of fact, I might join the S.S. myself. Bock could do with an assistant like me!"

First light was breaking as they made their way into Brussels. There was already quite a bit of market and factory traffic about, for the Belgians are early risers, and they were able to mingle with the crowds.

Their rendezvous with Krunjes was a green-grocer's shop, but before going there, Merridew wanted to get in touch with the radio operator and arrange for a message to be sent to London.

The operator worked as a pianist in a café, and that was the first destination. It took nearly an hour to get into the centre and find it, a smart-looking place just off the Avenue Louise. It was closed, but through the glass doors they could see the chairs piled on the tables and a man washing the floors.

"Wait on the other side of the street," said Merridew. "If anything goes wrong, just walk off quietly; find your way to the greengrocer's. Then the rest will be up to you and Krunjes."

Sherwood waited uneasily, looking in the shop windows, half expecting to see Delacroix's heavy features staring out at him, but a few minutes later Merridew rejoined him.

"He's not there," he snapped. "He's gone to Charleroi and won't be back until this afternoon. I wonder why he's gone there. I hope everything's all right. Anyhow, I shall have to come back, I suppose, but I don't like it much."

He was rather put out and silent as they made their way to the greengrocer's shop, which was in a shabby street behind the Midi Station.

The greengrocer—Jeanmaire, by name—was unloading a hand-cart when they arrived. He was a nervous, breathless little man, and had been expecting them ever since the arrival of the Ostend train, several hours earlier. The wait had not done him much good. He slammed the front door and rushed them up to his flat over the shop.

"More than welcome!" he rattled, "friends of dear Paul Krunjes. . . . Upstairs out of sight. . . . Never be too careful!"

It was a very expensively-furnished flat. Either Jeanmaire was an unusually successful green-grocer, or else he had a more profitable sideline— probably helping "dear Paul Krunjes."

"Krunjes has gone out . . . left a message . . . return to-night for you . . . stay here . . . rest and some food."

The room seemed suddenly very stuffy and Sherwood's arm was throbbing. The thought of food turned him over. He stripped off his leather jacket painfully and sank down gratefully into the most comfortable armchair going.

Merridew stared at him anxiously. "Your arm, laddie? I'll have a look at it, then you'd better get some sleep."

The wound did not look very good when the bandage was removed. It was red and swollen. The German sergeant at De Haan had not done the job properly and it was obviously infected. Merridew bathed it with hot water and Jeanmaire produced some antiseptic and fresh bandages. After that, feeling a bit easier, Sherwood settled down and went fast asleep with no trouble at all.

When he awoke, it was late afternoon. Merridew was already muffling himself up to go out.

"Any better?" he asked.

Sherwood stretched his arm, and wished he had not. It was less painful, but felt like lead.

"Well, you stay here," said Merridew. "I'm going back to the café, but we'd better go over the details of what you saw on that railway wagon so that the radio message can be as useful as possible."

"No, I'm coming with you," Sherwood said determinedly; the idea of staying behind, wondering what was happening was not very attractive, even though he disliked the whole business of going back to the café and knew that Merridew was uncomfortable about it too.

"Three things we know," said Merridew thoughtfully when they were out in the street, "the first is that these projectiles are not made in the Ardennes, they are sent there. That sentry said that he had been with the train since it left Essen, which is where the big German armament works are. The other points are that Yves's Resistance group is unreliable and that old Lepic is dead. Ten-to-one the Germans will put a decoy in his place to nab any of our agents sent there. I must stop that by letting Colonel Nick know."

They approached the café warily and strolled past it a few times on the opposite side of the street to make sure the coast was clear. They were not conspicuous because the evening rush of workers on their way home had already started. The café lights were on, but the blackout curtains had not yet been drawn, so they could see inside quite well. There were a few people sitting at the tables, but business was not brisk. At the far end, on a platform, a pianist was trying to liven up the proceedings. He had his back towards them so that all they could see was a bulging velvet jacket and a mop of greasy black hair. Every time the door swung open they heard him tinkling away like mad.

"That must be the chap," muttered Merridew. "If he can send wireless messages like he can play the piano, this shouldn't take long. You hang on here, laddie."

Sherwood looked up and down as Merridew crossed and was about to slip back into a doorway for shelter when he suddenly knew that his feeling about not returning to the café had been right. For, hurrying down the street from the Avenue Louise was the bulky figure of Delacroix. He was fairly belting along, his head tucked down as he dodged through the other pedestrians.

There was only one thing for it. Sherwood did not hesitate but dashed across the street and grabbed Merridew's arm just as he reached the entrance. One glance at Sherwood's face and he did not argue.

They hurried round the corner, up a service passage at the side, as though on their way to a fire. They did not know it, but that was exactly what they were on their way to. They were just in time, for Delacroix rushed past the end of the passage and turned in at the café.

Merridew gave a low whistle. "That was a close one! Let's see what the blighter's up to."

Standing well back in the shadows, they peered through a side window. It did not give a very clear view, but it was enough. Delacroix marched across the café, shoving the doorman and waiters aside, straight up to the pianist and fetched him a crack across the head that sent the man sprawling. He bounded up and dived on Delacroix. They rolled across the floor, fighting like wildcats, scattering chairs, tables and customers in all directions.

"We'd better get our chap away," rapped Merridew; but before they could move, a door at the back of the café burst open and in stormed Captain Bock at the head of an S.S. squad, and dragged the two men apart.

Bock was beside himself with rage. He stormed and raved at Delacroix, who was sitting on the floor trying to get his wind back.

"Saboteur!" he screamed. "You have ruined everything! Do you think the Englishman will come now? *Abwehr* pig!"

"But this man——?" gasped Delacroix, waving a podgy hand at the pianist.

"—is one of my men. The radio operator is under arrest. I warned Colonel Schieffen that the Englishman had been here this morning—and I was putting one of my men in his place." Bock brandished his fist at Delacroix, who gaped at him, open-mouthed. "If you interfere again," bawled Bock, "I'll have you shot. If you dare go near the greengrocer's, I'll shoot you myself. I'll . . . I'll . . ."

His cries of rage were drowned by the rush of customers for the door. They were quite prepared to enjoy a fight between another customer and the pianist, but if the S.S. were going to join in, that was another matter.

Merridew nudged Sherwood. "Out!" he rapped, "fast!"

They slipped into the street and lost themselves in the crowd.

"Did you hear what Bock said?" demanded Merridew savagely when they were clear. "He's on to Jeanmaire. We daren't go back to the shop— it's bound to be under watch. Delacroix's stupidity saved us from one trap to-night, but we can't count on that again."

"But what about Krunjes?"

"Yes—what about Krunjes. I tell you what I'll do, I'll try phoning the shop. There's a chance Jeanmaire will have some news and in any case we owe him a warning. It's the least we can do."

They chose another café, this time not far from the station. Merridew went into the phone-booth while Sherwood sat down in a dark corner and ordered some coffee.

Merridew came out in a few minutes, frowning. "Jeanmaire knew," he said grimly. "He was just getting out when I rang. He had a couple of spotters on the lookout for anything suspicious, and they reported that the shop was put under surveillance just after we left."

"What about Krunjes, then?" asked Sherwood again.

"Jeanmaire hasn't a clue where he is. All he knows is that Krunjes was to pick us up to-night. But he's not waiting to see what happens, and I can't say I blame him, either." Merridew relapsed into gloomy silence and sat toying with his cup of artificial coffee until it was cold, which did not matter much, for it was almost undrinkable, anyhow.

Sherwood did not want to add to Merridew's worries, but by this time he knew that his arm was in real trouble. It was aching and throbbing like a bad tooth, and he was feeling dizzy and feverish.

"I've got it!" said Merridew suddenly. "We'll save Krunjes yet, but we'll need a car." He tossed a few coins on the table and dragged Sherwood out into the street. Without further explanation he led the way towards the station.

In the road outside there were several unattended cars, most of them bearing German Service markings. There was no petrol for private motoring, and all cars had to be on some sort of official business.

He stopped beside a small Opel and tried the door.

"This one will do," he whispered. "It's not locked. Hop in!"

The lack of an ignition-key did not bother him. He reached under the dash and tore the cables loose. Then he joined two exposed ends and tried the starter. The engine came to life without hesitation.

"Keep your fingers crossed, laddie," he grinned. "We're in business again!"

"What now?" Sherwood asked as they headed towards Jeanmaire's shop.

"I can't explain now, just do as I say. I'm going to put you down at this end of the street and drive on to the other end. You stay there and keep your eyes open to cut Krunjes off if he comes from your direction."

Sherwood looked at the empty streets doubtfully. Once away from the main thoroughfares, there was hardly a soul about. Most of the shops and houses had their shutters down and were blacked out. The place looked deserted.

"We'll be spotted right away if Bock's men are watching," he protested.

"Don't worry, I'm going to create a diversion," said Merridew. "Here, take these." He took one hand off the wheel, felt inside his pocket and produced four fountain-pens. At least, they looked to Sherwood like fountain-pens.

"Look at the top of them—you'll see two red lines. Twist the caps round until the lines join." Sherwood did as he said and gave them back. "Right! Now you get out here and into a doorway; then keep your eyes skinned, because in a few minutes there'll be a crowd gathering, I promise you!"

Merridew pulled up at the corner of Jeanmaire's street and Sherwood ducked hurriedly into a darkened entrance. The Opel accelerated away until it came opposite to the shop, then slowed down for an instant. There was a tinkling of glass. The car picked up speed again, and disappeared smartly out of the other end of the street.

Nothing happened. Sherwood stood there shivering, wishing that his head would stop spinning and that he was somewhere else. Then, with a roar, the front of the shop blew out and an intense white fire was burning in its place. The light from it was blinding. Within minutes it spread all over the ground-floor and spilled out on to the pavement.

At once, from places of concealment along the

street, Bock's men came running into the road-way. Much good it did them, for one thing was certain: Krunjes would not be paying a call on Jeanmaire on that or any other evening.

They gathered helplessly in front of the fire and were soon joined by people from adjoining houses. In no time at all a crowd had gathered and Sher-wood heard Bock yelling for the street to be cleared.

There were soon so many people that the danger was not that Krunjes would be trapped, he was too fly to hang around once he had caught sight of the S.S., but that Merridew and Sherwood would lose track of him altogether.

Sherwood shoved his way over to a kiosk, try-ing to keep his left arm out of harm's way. From the low, flat roof there would be a better chance of keeping watch.

He tried, but it was no good—it was impossible to pull himself up. His arm was useless. The crowd surged as a fire-engine forced its way through and he was slammed back against the kiosk. Blinding pain shot up his arm and he staggered away to get clear, not caring where he was going, and nearly fell under the wheels of a small green van creeping through the crowd.

A furious bullet-head appeared out of the driver's window and he could have yelled with relief as he recognised the scarlet features of the driver. Krunjes was out of the van in a flash.

"Merridew . . . other end of the street . . . waiting for you," Sherwood managed to croak and then passed flat out.

CHAPTER TEN

THE S.S. TAKE OVER

By THE TIME they got on to Krunjes's barge Sherwood was delirious and needing medical attention pretty badly.

Krunjes rose to the occasion and produced a doctor who pre-war had done running repairs for the smugglers, after their brushes with the Customs and Police. He was a furtive, sour, little man, who complained bitterly because Krunjes forced him to stay on board until Sherwood's arm was mending.

The journey was spun out for over a week and by the time they reached Namur, where the doctor left them, Sherwood was on his feet again—a bit groggy and with a stiff arm, but definitely better.

Some time after they had left Namur behind, Merridew came down into the stuffy, cramped cabin and squatted on the bunk.

"I'm not sorry to lose *him*," he commented. " Still, he did his job well enough. It was a wonder that Krunjes found anyone to help us under the circumstances. What I should have done without him, I have no idea; he has been a real brick.

Among other things he arranged for my radio message to be taken to Charleroi and transmitted to London by our man there. He's been worth his weight in gold, has Krunjes."

"I know," said Sherwood feelingly. "He's the one stroke of luck we've had. It's a pity we shall soon have to part company with him. Where will he put us ashore—do you know yet?"

Merridew looked away abruptly as though the question embarrassed him.

"We've a cargo of cement for the Project 38 installation aboard. Yes, he's even thought of that. When we off-load, I—we shall smuggle ourselves ashore. I don't know whether it will work, but that's the plan."

Sherwood could feel that something was wrong, but as Merridew clearly did not want to talk about it, he did not press him but stared thoughtfully out of the cabin window.

They were passing through Dinant in the wooded valley of the River Meuse. An ancient citadel, grim reminder of other wars, towered high above them, against an overcast sky. The river was becoming congested with traffic to the installation which, from Latour's description, was now only a few miles farther up.

Underneath his rising excitement, as they approached their goal, Sherwood was uneasy about Merridew, who sat silently packing some provisions. Once ashore, they would be within the security area, where food would be hard to come by and they had decided to take some hardtack stowed inside their jackets in case they had to live in the forests for several days.

Sherwood had just about made up his mind to ask Merridew flatly what was worrying him, when Krunjes stuck his head down through the hatch.

"Boche police-boats," he announced disgustedly. "Keep below, boys; three men on one barge —too many, eh? I go slow up to the jetties to see if I can put you ashore somewhere, Merry. It will be dark enough in about an hour."

Merridew nodded without speaking. It occurred to Sherwood that he had not been included in this one-sided conversation.

"What did he mean 'put you ashore'?" he demanded suspiciously. "What about me?"

Merridew's expression changed to one almost of relief.

"I wasn't going to tell you until the last minute, laddie," he said quietly, "you're not coming with me. You're going straight on to Switzerland with Krunjes. He's agreed to take you."

Sherwood stared in amazement.

"Not coming with you!" he echoed. "But why? This is the part of the job I was sent for, isn't it?"

"I know that, but you're not fit enough yet, and

we can't hang around until you are. There was a reply to my radio message. London thinks we're taking too long as it is and wants a report as soon as possible."

"But my arm is almost healed. There's no . . ."

"Look," Merridew interrupted savagely, "I hate doing this. I need you with me, but if you cracked up ashore, it would be the end of both of us, and more important, of the job as well. You'd be an added risk in this condition. You're going on with Krunjes, laddie, and that's an order!"

Before Sherwood could reply, Krunjes's head reappeared. "We've arrived," he hissed. "But there's trouble on the jetties. Better take a look."

Sherwood clenched his fists. He did not relish going into the lion's den, but he was keyed-up for this job which they had come so far to do. Added to that, he had had all along the uncomfortable feeling of being just a passenger. Merridew had arranged everything, had taken all the decisions and more than a fair share of the risks.

As he followed Merridew over to the half-opened hatch, Sherwood made up his mind that whatever happened he was not going to be left behind.

The first glimpse of the installation was pretty breath-taking, and he knew that what he was seeing was only the water-side storage area. The valley side had been blasted away, exposing a near-

vertical rock-face. The space thus cleared at the
foot had been surfaced to form a vast platform on
which stood row upon row of store-sheds stretching out to the forest on either flank. From the
river side of the platform, which was just above
water level, jutted timber jetties lined with laden
barges. Mobile cranes and mechanical transporters were stationed along the jetties, waiting
to transfer the cargoes to the sheds.

Merridew whistled softly.

"If this is just the storage area, the Jerries are
certainly taking Project 38 seriously enough," he
muttered grimly. "Where's the trouble you were
talking about, Krunjes?"

"There's nothing happening on the jetties," said
Krunjes, "nothing goes on. You can't see from
down there, but many men are on the jetties.
Prisoners who unload, but they do nothing—just
stand. There is trouble. I smell it!"

As they swung round to come up into a vacant
berth, they had a clear view and saw what he was
talking about. Squads of men were gathered in
sullen groups round the cranes and transporters,
staring angrily along the jetty towards the
platform. They were a tough, ugly-looking crew.
Here and there a tattered French Army uniform
was recognisable, but for the most part they were
dressed in a ragged assortment of civilian clothes.
They were guarded by German soldiers, who

carried machine-pistols and looked as fed up as their charges. The reason was apparent, for lined up across the shoreward end of the jetty was a file of the now-familiar black-uniformed S.S.

Krunjes dodged down into the cabin. "It was that doctor," he snarled. "He betrayed us. I should not have let him go at Namur. I should have . . ." he drew his forefinger savagely across his throat to show what he should have done.

"I doubt it," said Merridew, "there's more to it than that. I don't know who's winning the war, but it looks as though the S.S. are beating the *Abwehr* for the control of German security. Look over there——" He pointed across the platform to where a group of S.S. officers were gathered, arguing with a tall, thin figure in field-grey.

"That's Colonel Schieffen," exclaimed Sherwood.

"And *Haupsturmfuhrer* Bock, and the wretched Delacroix. The whole circus!" added Merridew.

The argument seemed to be between Schieffen and a fair-haired S.S. officer They were too far off for them to overhear until the Colonel broke away angrily.

"I tell you, Schellenberg," he shouted, "the Project is a military weapon and I shall remain responsible for its security until the Führer orders otherwise. You can take charge of the prisoners, the stores and the jetties, but the inner compound, the technical site, is my responsibility. Is that clear?"

He stamped away to the other side of the platform, with Delacroix lumbering after him.

"Schellenberg is a top Nazi," whispered Merridew. "I told you, he's one of the heads of S.S. Intelligence."

The S.S. group broke up, laughing and congratulating the fair-haired officer who remained for a while in conversation with Bock, then he disappeared, leaving Bock in charge. Bock strode importantly towards the S.S. ranks, while Schieffen, white with rage, watched him.

"Before unloading begins," bawled Bock to his men, "I want these barges searched. You will examine stores during unloading, and then you will search each of the prisoners when it is finished."

That created a bit of a stir and no mistake. The prisoners shuffled their feet and groaned, and one or two brighter ones at the back even started booing. If they intended annoying Bock, they certainly succeeded.

"Silence!" he screamed. "Silence, you French swine! I will . . ."

"Captain Bock," rapped Colonel Schieffen, his voice like a knife, "these men have been working without food for twelve hours. It is time for them to return to camp. Unloading is finished for to-day."

Bock whipped round. "I am now in charge, Colonel, and these swine will take my orders! They will finish work when I say so. From now on we will have the utmost efficiency. You heard the orders of *Brigadefuhrer* Schellenberg."

The shouting and jeering of the prisoners almost drowned his voice. Then Bock did what turned out to be a foolish thing: he rushed across the jetty, seized a rather under-sized Frenchman by the throat and shook him like a rat.

It was the spark that caused the explosion. Four years in a prison camp, being pushed around, under-fed, overworked, was enough for anyone, and finally to have Bock served up on top was obviously more than the Frenchmen could stomach.

Like one man they turned on their guards and, without a shot being fired, disarmed them; then they went for the S.S., who were unable to open fire without hitting Bock.

Merridew turned to Sherwood grimly: "You need not worry about not going ashore now, laddie. If Bock searches the barges he's bound to recognise Krunjes and me. We must make a break while we can. Come on!"

Krunjes grunted assent and the three of them swarmed over the edge of the jetty.

The S.S. and guards had their hands too full to notice them in the general free-for-all. Once on the jetty, Sherwood could see that there were many more prisoners-of-war involved than he had realised. Other squads, who had been working in the store-sheds, and assembled on the platform waiting to go back to their camp, promptly joined in the fight. Some of them were piling on to the barges, trying to escape by water, while others were fighting their way ashore to break out into the forest. One or two in desperation just hurled themselves into the water, hoping to swim to freedom.

"Keep together," yelled Merridew over his shoulder to the other two as they charged into the milling crowd and forced their way through. They did not get very far, though. A machine-gun opened up, firing tracers just over their heads. An armoured car pulled out from between two sheds and raced across the platform, to block the end of the jetty.

After that, their part of the mutiny folded up abruptly. Even the desperate courage of the Frenchmen could not stand up to an armoured car. The S.S. lost no time in rounding up those who had not already got away. They were rushed across the platform and booted aboard a line of lorries.

"We are out of the frying-pan all right, laddie,"

panted Merridew in Sherwood's ear, "and we haven't landed in a bed of roses, either!"

"Silence!" roared one of the guards, and came for them with his rifle but before he could do anything, a diversion was created by the re-appearance of Bock. He had lost his cap and half his uniform, and was soaked to the skin into the bargain. He must have been pitched off the jetty in the fight, and the ducking had not improved his temper.

"Get them back to the camp," he screeched. "Have them on the parade-ground. Every man on the parade-ground!" He caught sight of the still-immaculate Schieffen who was standing to one side with Delacroix, watching with a con-temptuous sneer on his thin features, and rushed away furiously out of sight.

The loaded lorry started up and pulled away across the platform on to a road leading out to the forest.

It was difficult to see very much, for there were three S.S. guards sitting on the tail-board just looking for an excuse to start shooting.

After half a mile or so, running between the store-sheds, they checked out through a heavily-fortified defence post. The lorries changed into low gear and ground slowly up a sharp incline. At the top there was a glimpse of the great ex-panse of forest before they plunged downwards, through two more check-points set in walls of barbed-wire, into the prisoner-of-war camp. They were ordered out and found themselves on the edge of a parade-ground in the middle of groups of timber huts. They were formed up into three rows and left standing there to await the arrival of the rest of the prisoners.

The S.S. guards ignored them and busily discussed something among themselves, probably the progress of the feud with the *Abwehr*.

"I know these parts," croaked Krunjes as they took stock of their surroundings. "That stone hut, I know—I have used it before the war."

Sherwood looked in the direction indicated and saw, on the farther side of the barbed-wire, part of what appeared to be a ruined hunting-lodge. It had been re-roofed and stood half-hidden among the trees. Earth was banked up around it, suggesting that it was now used as an explosives store.

"If we get the chance," rasped Krunjes, "make for that, eh?"

Merridew and Sherwood both nodded silently. It did not look to Sherwood as though they would have much chance of making for anywhere. They were pretty well hemmed in and overlooked by guard-towers standing fifty-feet high at intervals along the fence.

They appeared to be in the middle one of the

three zones Latour had told them about. The zones were separated by continuous barbed wire. The outer one, where the stone hut was, contained the quarters of the German troops. In the middle zone, where they were standing, were the prisoners' camps. The inner zone was hidden by rising ground which had been cleared of trees.

Sherwood felt his pulse quicken as he stared at that bare slope. He knew that beyond lay the secret they had come so far to find: for the inner zone must contain Project 38.

All this time, men were pouring on to the parade-ground from the huts and lorries arriving from the jetties.

Merridew nudged him. "Don't stare about like a new arrival, laddie," he whispered. "You're supposed to have been here a long time!"

Sherwood was about to reply, when he caught sight of Bock arriving, followed by Colonel Schieffen and Delacroix. Bock was blue with cold and still dripping wet.

"Get them lined up," he shouted to his men, "and keep the dock-workers separate from the rest."

The S.S. dashed about, forming up the men who had not been working on the jetty so that the parade-ground was lined on three sides around Bock, with the squads from the jetties, including Merridew, Sherwood and Krunjes, in front of him. They kept as far back as they could. There did not seem much danger of being recognised, for there must have been at least five hundred prisoners on the parade-ground, and the light was going.

Bock did not waste any time in getting to the point.

"I want every fifth man from the dock company out in front," he barked.

His men ran along the ranks, numbering the prisoners off. Sherwood received a violent shove in the back which sent him staggering forward, through the front rank, straight into Delacroix, who stared at him without a flicker of recognition. His relief at this narrow escape was short-lived, however, when he realised that he had been separated from Merridew and Krunjes.

The prisoners who had fallen out—about thirty men—were immediately surrounded by S.S. and marched up in front of Bock.

"I've had you assembled," he bawled, turning his head from side to side, so that everyone on the parade-ground could get the benefit, "to tell you that you are now under the command of the S.S."

This was greeted by subdued booing and cat-calls.

"I'm going to teach you what that means," he yelled furiously. "I'm going to show you what

German discipline is. These dock-workers have tried to mutiny. I'm going to make an example of them. You will assemble here again at first light to-morrow to witness their punishment. As a warning to the rest of you, these men here in front will then be shot!"

CHAPTER ELEVEN

PRISONERS' REVOLT

THE DEAD silence following Bock's announcement was broken by renewed booing, but this time the S.S. were ready, and the noise died away under the threat of their machine-guns. The thirty condemned prisoners were hustled through the check-point to the outer zone, where they were locked in a store-shed near the main guard-room.

When the door was slammed, leaving them in darkness, it was for Sherwood the worst moment of the whole operation. For several minutes his fellow prisoners seemed too stunned by this disaster to speak, and he was able to hear that the entire camp outside was again in an uproar. Then everyone started shouting at once, hurling abuse at the S.S. and calling to see whether any of their friends were in the shed.

The row went on until one voice, louder than the others, shouted for order:

"Shut up and listen to me, lads. This is Sergeant Perier. We won't get anywhere shouting our heads off, and we're not going to give in without a fight."

136

There was a rumbled chorus of agreement.

"That's right, then. We've got nothing to lose, now. If we're going to be shot, we'll take some of the Boches with us! Let's see where we are. Has anyone got a light?"

Sherwood had some matches and decided that, as everyone knew and apparently trusted Perier, there was no point in trying anything on his own. He handed the matches over.

The walls and floor were gone over carefully. They were concrete and with no weak spots anywhere. It would have taken pneumatic drills or sledge-hammers to make a hole in them. That left the roof, but it was of corrugated sheeting and there was no hope there, either.

"If we can't get out through the floor, the roof or the walls, there's nothing else for it, lads, we'll have to get out through the door," said Perier at last. "Any ideas?"

There was a pause before someone piped up:

"How's this, Sergeant—some of us could get up on the roof ties, then the rest could make such a row that the Boches will have to see what's going on, and we could jump them."

"That's a good one!" jeered another voice. "The Boches will just stick a machine-gun through the door and mow the lot of us down!"

"We'll have a look," said Perier.

The roof ties were metal rods spanning the shed,

holding the rafters in place. They were strong enough to support several men, but would give no concealment. It was a pretty forlorn chance, but Perier said: "If that's all we can do, we'll try it."

It was decided to wait until after "lights-out" had sounded so that only the Germans on duty would be about. That meant waiting for several hours, but the escape plan was not yet complete. Even if the break-out succeeded, they would still be in the outer zone and penned in by barbed-wire.

"We'll have to organise this," said Perier. "The first thing will be to get some arms, the second to set the lads free from the prison camp, and the third to take the check-point covering the gate to the forest. After that, it will be every man for himself—if we get that far!"

After some argument, it was agreed that every-one should rush the nearby guard-room, which had an armoury attached, and then split into two parties, to liberate the prisoners' camp and to open the attack on the outer check-point.

"Now, if that's settled," said Perier, "just keep quiet until I give the word. We don't want to alert the Boches too soon. Let them think we're not going to give any trouble."

The racket in the camp was still going on. Bock had really stirred the prisoners up, and they were ready for a fight, given the chance. They chanted and hammered on their huts to express their disgust at the S.S., but without arms there was nothing more they could do.

The long wait gave Sherwood an opportunity of thinking things over. Even if the break-out succeeded, it would be difficult to find Merridew and Krunjes in the confusion. He decided finally that the thing would be to make for the old hunting-lodge and hope that they would do the same.

That was the rub. It was all very well for Perier to talk about attacking the check-points, but the chances were that the open ground would be swept by machine-guns both from the check-points and the fifty-feet high watch-towers. It occurred to Sherwood that half their problems would be solved if one of the towers could be seized at the outset.

He crawled over to Perier and suggested it. The Frenchman struck a match and stared at him suspiciously. During this examination, "lights-out" was sounded.

"Good idea," grunted Perier. "We'll try one of the towers together, if you're game. I'd like to get my hands on a machine-gun again. We had better make a start, then." He stood up. "On your feet, lads. The six men detailed, up on the roof ties. Then the rest of you at the back of the shed so the Boches will have to come right inside to see what's going on. When I give the word, bawl your heads off, but shut up when they come."

He grabbed Sherwood's arm. "You stay with me, lad—we'll keep behind the door. If it works, we'll lead the rush on the guard-room."

When the six men were in place, the rest crowded as far back as they could. Sherwood crouched with Perier behind the door.

"Right!" barked Perier, "let's have it!"

Immediately everyone yelled at the top of their voices, until in the confined space the row was deafening. After a few minutes there was a pause and the German sentry outside could be heard hammering on the door and shouting for silence.

"Again, lads," ordered Perier. "Keep it up!"

There was a second uproar, followed by a third and a fourth. In the intervals there were answering yells from the prisoners' camp and blasts on the German sentry's whistle as he called for the guard to turn out.

Encouraged by this, Sherwood's companions shouted louder than ever, until finally the door flew open, flattening him and Perier against the wall. Three Germans burst in, carrying torches, with sub-machine-guns slung at the "ready," followed by the guard commander.

"So, you can't wait till the morning to be shot," the guard commander roared, playing the beam of his torch over the men crouching against the rear wall.

Sherwood felt Perier tense beside him. They

waited breathlessly to see whether the men on the roof ties would be spotted.

"There are worse ways of dying, than being shot," continued the German N.C.O., gaining confidence at the sudden silence, "as you will discover unless you keep quiet."

It was the last threat he ever uttered. With a roar, Perier sprang forward, slamming the door and diving at the nearest German. The men on the roof ties dropped like stones out of the darkness.

The torches went out; the guns flared, followed by screams as bullets found some of the prisoners. But in a few minutes it was over. The Germans, even with their sub-machine-guns, were no match for thirty desperate men, in the darkness.

"Outside," bawled Perier, "to the guard-room!"

With surprise on the prisoners' side, the speed of the attack gave the Germans no time to recover, and the men on the watch-towers did not realise what was going on in time to stop them. The captured sub-machine-guns flushed out the rest of the guard, and they were through the guard-room into the armoury.

"Get yourself a gun apiece," shouted Perier above the din. "Be careful to take the right ammunition."

There was a bit of a hold-up because the armoury was stacked with gas-masks. Several minutes passed before any guns and ammunition-boxes were found. Sherwood grabbed a machine-pistol and a box of grenades, and followed Perier to the door.

"The first six of you keep the outer check-point busy," ordered Perier, "the rest break through into the prison camp. I'll try to cover you from one of the towers. Get going!"

Outside, the Germans were still uncertain what had happened. The searchlights on the towers were probing aimlessly, while the machine-guns poured tracers down on to the prisoners' huts. The ricochets rocketed wildly up into the darkness like sparks from a fire.

"We'll take the tower nearest the gate into the camp," Sherwood suggested, and Perier grunted agreement.

Doubled up, the pair of them raced across the space towards the tower. Half-way across, a searchlight caught them. They were right in the open, with no possibility of cover, so they kept straight on. A second machine-gun opened up, filling the air with tracers and kicking up the earth around them.

As Sherwood reached the foot of the tower, he plunged into the darkness again. The search-light mounting did not permit a 90^0 depression, so he was safe for the time being, and flung himself down beside the barbed-wire fence to look round for Perier. But the Frenchman was not to be seen. The beam moved back to reveal him crawling on all fours but, as the machine-guns stuttered into life, he leapt to his feet, staggered a few paces forward into a stream of tracers, and fell face downwards. He did not move again.

Sherwood found that he was shaking all over and steeled himself to think what his next move should be. Alone, it was impossible to attack the tower. To scale the ladder, without covering fire to keep the Germans' heads down, was out of the question.

The searchlight beam swept on again, towards the gate of the prison camp. The attack was making no progress and it was clear that unless the main body of prisoners were freed quickly, the break-out would be overwhelmed by the Germans who were already rallying.

Sherwood had decided to move along the wire and try to get within grenade distance of the check-point at the gate, when a better idea struck him: The towers were supported by four timber legs, braced at intervals by cross-members, forming a lattice right up to the platform carrying the searchlight and machine-gun. If the grenades would fracture one of the timber supports, the whole structure might come down, tearing a gap in the wire. It was worth a try, although he knew that grenades were far from ideal for the job.

He scraped a hole beside a support, and laid all the grenades—about a dozen—except one, hard against the timbers; then he ripped the pin from the one he had put aside, stuffed it among the others and shot off in the direction of the hunting-lodge. He counted to five, flung himself down and covered his head. The ground jolted sharply as the grenades blasted off. For several seconds it looked as though the support was still intact. Then, the searchlight began to move. Slowly at first, but with gathering speed, it fell, still blazing, through a wide arc as the whole tower toppled over.

The Germans on the platform came down yelling as they were plunged into space. The tower landed with a splintering crash, dead along the wire and the searchlight went out, accompanied by loud cheering from the camp. The outer searchlights swivelled round to cover the gap in the wire, but the party attacking the check-point at the inner gate, promptly concentrated on shooting them out.

As the first wave of prisoners poured from the huts straight for the gap, Sherwood made off again towards the hunting-lodge. It was well out of the line of the battle, which rapidly took shape as the prisoners came through the wire and joined the attack on the outer check-point guarding the main gate to the forest.

It was an anxious wait because Merridew and Krunjes might well have joined in the general break-out. Several groups ran by, silhouetted against the beam of the remaining searchlights, but Merridew and Krunjes were not among them.

When they did arrive, they came silently, under cover. The first Sherwood knew about it was Merridew calling his name from the shadows at the back of the lodge.

Krunjes appeared and slapped him on the back. "Good boy," he boomed. "Now we get into the lodge—quick!"

"It covers the entrance to a cave leading up into the hills," explained Merridew. "Krunjes used it for smuggling operations before the war."

"A business depot," chuckled Krunjes, wrestling with the padlock on the stout door. "If we get into it, we can come out higher up and miss the mine-fields. When it is light we shall see over the inner zone, eh?"

The lodge was a simple one-room affair, intended as sleeping quarters for hunting-parties. The Germans had not only turned it into a store, they had paved over the earth floor, sealing off the entrance to the cave. Krunjes stamped angrily in the corner where it had been. "There used to be a wooden trap-door," he growled. "I should have known they would not have left it. What do we do now?"

It was a good question, because they had left it rather late to join the break-out. Judging by the firing in the forest, some of the prisoners were already through.

Only the check-point at the main gate was preventing the escape becoming general, and that was being hotly engaged by prisoners still holding the main guard-room and armoury. The ground in front of the lodge was being swept by fire.

"We'll try lifting the paving," said Merridew. "We can't give up now. You keep watch, laddie."

Sherwood stationed himself by the door while the others set to, scraping out the cement from the joints.

The Germans were just calling off an attempt to storm the guard-room in the face of a barrage of grenades and returning to cover behind the check-point. The reason soon became apparent, for an 88-mm. field-gun, mounted on a tracked chassis, ground up to the check-point and traversed round until it was aimed point-blank at the guard-room.

"It is murder!" muttered Krunjes grimly. "They won't have a chance."

The prisoners in the guard-room, realising the desperate position, stepped up their firing, but much of it was wild as the check-point was throwing everything it had at them, to cover the gun.

The gun team worked furiously. Sherwood

thought for a second that the bulky figure of Delacroix was among them but, in the reflected glare of the last searchlight still in action, it was difficult to be certain.

"Get down," he said. "There may be splinters."

The explosion, when it came, was deafening. The ground shuddered and the lodge shook as though about to collapse over their heads.

No gun that Sherwood had ever heard had fired like that. As the dust and smoke blew away, he was staggered to see the guard-room still standing.

"The gun!" exclaimed Merridew, "the gun's blown itself up and the gate with it!"

It was true. The long barrel was sagging drunkenly over the remains of the shattered checkpoint and the gate had disappeared completely, leaving the way clear out to the forest. The prisoners streamed from the guard-room, wasting no time in taking advantage of their luck.

"The breech-block must have gone," guessed Sherwood, "and the ammunition has gone up as well."

"Well, what shall we do?" demanded Merridew. "Shall we get out, too, while the going's good and try another approach through the forest?— What do you think, Krunjes?"

There was no reply, so Merridew struck a match. Krunjes had disappeared. Where he had been standing the floor had caved in leaving a gaping black hole about four feet across.

The shock of the explosion had done their work for them in exposing the entrance to the cave, but what had it done to Krunjes? He soon answered this question himself as his familiar bullet-head, plastered with earth, reappeared out of the hole.

"Come, boys—the cave—quick!"

Merridew and Sherwood lost no time in following him into the cave and putting as much distance between them and the lodge as they could. The explosion of the "88" had given the Germans something to think about, but they dared not count on much of a breathing space.

The floor of the cave sloped sharply upwards and in places its rocky sides ran with water. Fortunately Krunjes knew it like the back of his hand, for there were branches and side shafts in which they might easily have lost themselves. Even so, it was rough going as sometimes the roof came down as low as three feet and the floor was strewn with rocks. It was a relief when at last the air freshened and they saw ahead the dim light of the night sky.

They thrust their way out through the undergrowth on to the side of a steep, wooded escarpment. Krunjes did not hesitate, but pushed on smartly uphill.

This part of the forest seemed completely

deserted and it was not until the next day that they knew the reason why. The slope became steeper and the going harder, and Sherwood wondered breathlessly whether Krunjes knew where he was leading them. Being laid up with a bullet wound had not been a good preparation for mountaineering.

Just when he had decided that he would have to stop for a breather, Krunjes halted and waited for the others to catch up. Then he pointed to an outcrop of rock fifty feet above.

"We stay up there until it is light," he said. "We used it as a lookout post before the war. You can see for miles and we shall overlook your famous Project 38."

"Right," agreed Merridew, "But if it's such a good observation-post the Germans may have manned it themselves, and we may be walking into a trap. You two wait here, and I'll make sure the coast is clear. I'll whistle for you to follow." He disappeared into the darkness, and a few minutes later a soft whistle came from up above.

After a sharp scramble up the last slope, Sherwood and Krunjes joined him among the rocks.

"There's no sign that anyone has been here for years," he said. "So we can make ourselves snug until we get our bearings."

"Snug" was hardly the word Sherwood would have chosen because, although they were sheltered from the wind, he could think of at least a dozen more comfortable places to spend a February night than a hill-top in the Ardennes. However, they had some hard biscuits and cheese which Krunjes had taken from the barge and were all glad enough of a break after the exertions of the last few hours.

Although their surroundings were masked by the darkness, they could see the searchlight still on in the prison camp far below and now and again heard bursts of firing from the forest near the river. Bock and his men were having a busy night.

Krunjes chuckled. "This is like the old days," he said. "I have spent many nights up here with a load of French 'merchandise,' waiting for the signal to go down to the depot. The sacristan of the church at the other side of the valley used to put a light in the tower when the coast was clear."

"Did you ever get caught?" inquired Merridew cheerfully. He always seemed in the best of humours after a narrow escape.

"Caught? No, but the sacristan did. He was a good boy, though. Me, I was lucky."

"Never luckier than to-night," said Merridew. "We would have been stuck in the lodge if that gun had not blown up. What do you think happened, laddie?"

"I don't know," replied Sherwood dully. To tell the truth the exercise had made him feel sleepy. "Maybe a faulty shell or damaged breech-block. Perhaps in the excitement one of the crew rammed the charge instead of the shell—it's happened before. It could have been Delacroix. I thought I saw him with the gun crew."

"Collaborator," growled Krunjes. "I would like to deal with that one myself." He explained in detail what he would do with all collaborators.

"Steady on, Krunjes," said Merridew. "He's not such a gift to the Jerries as all that. He's bungled everything he's done up to now. He missed an easy chance of spotting us in the cellar in Ostend and then he gave Bock's trap away in the café. And now he may have blown up a gun and set all the prisoners free. A few more collaborators like that, and the Germans would have to surrender."

"No matter. He is a traitor as well as a fool," grumbled Krunjes, beginning to be angry. "I would . . ."

Sherwood could have told him he was wasting his time letting Merridew provoke him, but was too tired to bother. They were still wrangling when he dropped off to sleep, propped between two rocks. His last thought was of Delacroix. Somehow the swarthy man had not looked like a blunderer in the brewery cellar. Sherwood had an uneasy feeling there was something he was missing, something to do with Delacroix, but before he could decide what it was, he was fast asleep.

When he awoke, the sun was coming up in a clear sky. In other circumstances it would have been a perfect day, but as he stamped about trying to restore his circulation he was in no mood to appreciate the weather. He was relieved to find that, apart from a few twinges in his arm, he felt none the worse for sleeping out.

Krunjes had disappeared and Merridew was lying full length, peering out between the rocks that had sheltered them.

"Come and have a look," called Merridew, "but keep your head down. Krunjes was right, we can see the whole bag of tricks from here—but what on earth it is, I have no idea."

Sherwood went over and crouched down beside him. It was certainly a spectacle. The object of their mission, Project 38, was spread out before them.

The inner zone was about a quarter-of-a-mile square. In the centre there was the hillock Latour had spoken of, covered by rows of what appeared to be massive ventilating shafts protruding a few feet above the surface. Around the base of the hill there were wide concrete-lined entrances screened by blast walls and entered by rail spurs, which sprang from a railhead near the boundary of the zone. Needless to say, there was a heavily fortified strong-point where the line passed out of sight into a steep-sided ravine. Near the entrances were low store-sheds flanked by more, heavily banked, blast walls. These sheds were connected by a system of overhead pipes and the pipes were painted the same bright yellow as the rail tanker they had seen in Brussels.

Although there were stacks of building materials within the enclosure, they appeared to be for quarters and out-buildings which were going up on the farther side of the hill, rather than for the underground installation. From the rather spacious layout, it looked as though the quarters were for officers and technicians who had to be on the spot all the time.

"What do you think they are for?" asked Merridew, pointing to the high ridge on the farther side of the enclosure where four steel pylons, about two hundred feet high, carried saucer-shaped structures.

"I don't know for sure, but they look as though they might be for transmitting wireless beams. They're moving slightly. Probably the saucers can be revolved to face any direction, something like our radar, perhaps."

Merridew grunted. "Well, laddie," he said, "this is it! We've got you this far, now we must get you into that underground place, so that you

can find out what it is all about. Krunjes is off
reconnoitring a way into the enclosure now, so
you'd better have something to eat, while you've
still the chance."

Project 38 was turning out to be more complicated than expected, and Sherwood was beginning
to doubt whether his artillery training would
be enough for him to understand it. However, it
was too late to do anything about that now, and
he set to, devouring the remainder of the biscuits
and cheese.

Before he had finished, Krunjes returned and
flung a coil of rope on the ground before sinking
down rather wearily.

"The Boches take no chance," he growled.
"There is an electrified fence, barbed-wire, and
minefield right round this inner part. We were
lucky last night. There were mines up along the
path we came. That is why it is so quiet here."

"There must be some way to get in," insisted
Merridew.

"Two ways," agreed Krunjes. "Two. There is
a road through the soldiers' camp and there is the
railway. The road is no good, eh? We try the
railway."

"We certainly can't go back through the camp,"
said Merridew. "You're right, we'll have to try
the railway, then."

They decided on working round to the ravine

and lying up under cover to see what happened when trains reached the check-point. They set off through the trees, avoiding any clearing and keeping their eyes skinned for booby-traps and mines. This was not too difficult, for the mines had been carelessly laid and were marked by tell-tale patches of bare earth.

"I thought you were going to leave us and push on to Switzerland," said Sherwood to Krunjes as they picked their way through the undergrowth.

Krunjes's scarlet face creased in a broad grin.

"I change my mind," he chuckled. "First, we play the Boches some bad jokes, eh?"

CHAPTER TWELVE

THE END OF PROJECT 38

BY LATE afternoon they were satisfied that the only
way of entering the inner zone was by smuggling
themselves in by rail. The rest of the day they
laid up under a big boulder half-way down the
ravine, watching the trains. There was an hourly
shuttle service on the narrow-gauge single track,
bringing in equipment and building materials.
The trains, pulled by small diesels, were halted and
searched at the check-point before running on to
the spurs inside the zone. Then the diesels were
unhitched and sent back to the main line railhead
with the empties.

They noted particularly that the empties were
not searched on the way out. That seemed important, because if they completed their mission
undetected, there would be an easy way of escape
open.

"We'll leave it as near dark as possible," said
Merridew, "but we don't want to miss the last
train."

Krunjes pointed to lights mounted on poles

beside the spurs. "Maybe they work at night, too."

"Perhaps," replied Merridew, "but we can't count on it, and in any case dusk will suit us best. It will be as light as day in there when those lights come on."

They decided that, once inside, they would make for the ventilators on the hill and that, if possible, Sherwood would try to get into the underground installation down one of the shafts.

As Merridew said: "We should be able to hear if extractor fans are working. If they are, then the ventilators are out. But they're worth a try because the entrances are pretty heavily guarded. I only hope they are ventilators. I counted up to nearly a hundred of them so there will be enough to choose from."

There seemed no chance of getting into the hill on a rail wagon, for, although a number of the spurs ran in through the entrances, no wagon went inside the whole time they were watching. All unloading was done in the open, which suggested that the underground works had already been completed.

"I, too, think it is finished," agreed Krunjes, who had just returned from scouting, "because I saw a company in white overalls marched into one entrance and five to ten minutes after another company marched out. These were technicians working in watches."

"Working in shifts, you mean," grinned Merri-dew. "We are not at sea now! So much the better if it is finished. It will be easier for you, laddie, to get an idea of what's going on."

He produced some more "fountain-pens" from his pocket. "You'd better have these, you might find a use for them."

Sherwood took them rather gingerly, remem-bering what the other "fountain-pens" had done in Jeanmaire's shop.

"They'll take longer than the others to go off," Merridew added encouragingly. "You know how to set them—just twist the tops till the lines join."

Sherwood stowed them cautiously inside his jacket. "How do they work?"

"When they're set, an acid starts eating through a metal wire inside—but never mind that now. I think we ought to try the next train. If we are separated, try to rendezvous by this rock. It's easy to pick out. Don't forget. O.K.? Let's go."

Krunjes and Sherwood followed him to the edge of the ravine. They had to find a spot where the bank was low enough for them to jump on to a wagon, when the train had stopped for inspection.

It was less difficult than expected, for the brush grew up to the edge of the cutting, which was about fifteen feet deep. They lay concealed near the edges for about twenty minutes before the next train halted below them. The four soldiers who inspected the wagons were in a hurry to get the job over.

"Wait until they pass round the back of the end wagon, then jump," whispered Merridew.

They managed it without trouble and slid under a tarpaulin covering bags of cement.

"Let us hope the rest is as easy. . ." chuckled Krunjes who appeared to be enjoying himself.

The soldiers walked back along the length of the train. A whistle blew and they moved slowly forward into the central zone. The diesel was unhitched and another shunted them from behind on to a spur where they were left standing. Everything was very quiet. The silence was unnerving; Sherwood thought he could almost feel the Germans preparing to pounce.

Merridew braced himself and lifted the tarpaulin enough to see over the side of the wagon. He looked round cautiously, then suddenly dropped flat again.

"Don't move," he snapped, "it's the S.S."

They waited, hardly daring to breathe. A squad of men marched by, their studded boots ringing on the concrete. Orders were shouted and Bock's unmistakable voice could be heard bawling above the others. Then the footsteps died away again.

Sherwood knew that they just had to move soon, for unloading could not be delayed much longer, and at any moment the lights overhead would come on, so he nudged Merridew impatiently to see if the coast was yet clear.

Merridew tried again. "O.K.," he whispered, "make straight for the hill, and keep down. The S.S. have patrols out."

One after the other they slipped over the end into the space between two wagons.

"Right. Sherwood first, off you go," said Merridew.

Keeping doubled up, Sherwood scurried towards the dark mass of the hill, hoping the others would not lose track in the dusk. He need not have worried. Krunjes came up behind, puffing and blowing, as he reached the first slope. As Merridew followed, the lights by the wagons came on, flooding the unloading area with light.

"Just in the nick of," panted Merridew. "Keep straight on, we can't stop now. But, for Pete's sake, keep your heads down."

The first row of ventilators stood out starkly against the sky above them. The slope was much steeper than it appeared from outside the zone and they were on hands and knees before they had finished.

Sherwood ran his hand cautiously round the rim of the nearest ventilator and found it blocked by a loose-fitting wooden plug, which came away quite easily, uncovering a circular hole nearly three feet in diameter.

"This can't be a ventilator," he said, uncertainly. "The metal must be at least nine inches thick."

"I know—it's more like a chimney," Merridew replied, and dropped a small stone in. They listened intently but did not hear it strike the bottom.

There was no point in hanging about. Every minute increased the danger of being seen by the patrols.

"I'll try this one," Sherwood decided, taking the rope which Krunjes had knotted into a bos'n's chair.

"Good lad," whispered Merridew. "If you get into trouble, give three clear tugs and we'll pull you up again. Here, you'd better take all the matches we've got."

With Krunjes's help, Sherwood settled the loop so that one hand and both feet would be free to fend off the sides of the shaft. One last check to make sure the "fountain-pens" were secure inside his jacket, and he raised his hand to show that he was ready. He took a deep breath himself, then slid off the rim, down into pitch darkness.

It seemed suddenly very quiet after the wind-swept hillside. There was no sound except for the creak of the rope. The sides of the shaft felt machine-smooth and without joints. Once or twice his hands passed over small circular holes, but he was dropping too quickly to investigate.

The pale disc of sky above dwindled as the length of rope above him lengthened rapidly. He was beginning to wonder whether the rope would run out before the bottom was reached, when his left foot caught in one of the holes, jerking him to a stop. The rope continued to come down, curling round his head and shoulders. He could not understand why the others did not stop paying it out, since they must have felt that his weight was no longer on it.

He looked up desperately and saw that the opening was brilliantly lit as though a search-light was trained across it. It suddenly blacked out and the rest of the rope came snaking down, nearly braining him.

Several minutes passed before he could dis-entangle it and let it drop away. Then he tried to take stock calmly. Obviously the others had been spotted, and feeling the rope go slack, had as-sumed that he had reached the bottom. They had thrown the rest of the coil down and replaced the cover before making off, so that it would be more difficult for the S.S. to find which shaft had been tampered with. So far so good, but that still left him trapped. The most important thing now was to find a way down, without the rope.

Bracing his back against the side, he bent his left leg slowly and felt with his right foot to see if there was another hole lower down. There was —directly in line with the first and about three feet lower; and again another, below that. He moved downwards steadily, but it was painfully slow and exhausting. During a stop for breath, he remembered the matches and cursed himself for not thinking of them before.

The interior of the shaft stretched up into the darkness, gleaming as though it were polished. Somehow it looked familiar. He had the odd feeling that he had seen it often before. Then panic swept over him in a sickening wave for he realised that he was trapped in the barrel of a gigantic gun.

He stayed without moving for a long time as, gradually, the whole of Project 38 began to take shape in his mind.

He knew that one of the chief problems with rockets was the amount of fuel needed to lift them into the air. Once up, it did not take much to keep them going. When they were used as weapons, the fuel took up much more space than the war-head and most of it was for the initial lift. If they could be fired from guns this difficulty would be overcome and a greater proportion of the projectile could be used for carrying explosives.

By using smooth bores, like the one he was in, the Germans would avoid the wear and tear in rifling, which shortened the life of most big guns. The retractable fins on the rockets were for stability, usually provided by the spinning effect caused by rifling, which consisted of corkscrew-like grooves along the inside of the barrel.

He did not know how much of this occurred to him at the time, but he already had a pretty good idea of what Project 38 was about, when there was a low rumbling just beneath his feet, and light flooded up from below. The great breech was being opened.

A hand appeared and collected the coiled rope on the open block. Someone whispered his name. The sound echoed eerily along the barrel. When he did not move it was repeated and a hand came up to grab his right foot.

He slid down out of the breech like a spent shell-case and crashed on to the concrete floor of a low chamber. Dazed by the fall and half blinded by the light, he found himself staring stupidly into the swarthy features of Delacroix, who was bending over him.

"Ah," wheezed Delacroix, "I guessed it would be you, Sherwood. I thought I should never find the right gun in time."

He hoisted Sherwood to his feet and urged him across the chamber to a narrow cupboard-like compartment. "There is no time for explanations. Just get in here and stay quiet until I return." The door slammed leaving Sherwood in complete darkness again, wondering whether it was all a lunatic nightmare. Why was Delacroix trying to rescue him—or was it just a trick to keep him quiet while Delacroix fetched the guard? Perhaps the *Abwehr* would want to hush up the fact that a British agent had managed to penetrate right into the Project in case the S.S. claimed that it was due to inefficiency and used it as another argument why they should take over the security. But how did Delacroix know his name?

The door opened and Delacroix thrust a bundle of white overalls into his arms.

"Change into these, then follow me. If we are stopped, you are a German technician who is opening the guns for me to make a security check. Remember!"

In spite of his confusion, Sherwood had a good look round the chamber while pulling on the overalls. There were five gun-breeches jutting down through the ceiling. Directly beneath them were metal link belts to carry up the rockets from below. To overcome the difficulty of loading into the vertical guns, electro-magnetic devices stood ready to hold the rockets in place until the breech-blocks were closed. Two massive cylinders, on either side of each barrel, appeared to be recupera-

tors for stabilising the guns after the shock of
firing.

"Hurry! Hurry!" Delacroix waddled back from
keeping watch at the entrance to the chamber.
"I will explain—but not here! There is no time.
Come!"

Sherwood followed out into a narrow, dimly-lit
gallery connecting a series of chambers similar
to the one they had just left. Delacroix
scurried along in front, his baggy grey uniform
making him look like a great toad in the half-
light.

The gallery must have been nearly a hundred
yards long and at the end opened out into a small
hall, with a bank of four lifts along one side.

Up till then the whole place had seemed deserted. But standing at the end of the hall, deep in
conversation, were two Army officers, one of
whom Sherwood instantly recognised as Colonel
Schieffen. The Colonel looked up as they came in
and barked at Delacroix: "Well, did you find
anything?"

"Nothing, *Herr Kolonel*," panted Delacroix. "I
have inspected all the guns in this gallery. There
is no sign of sabotage."

"You see," said the Colonel to the other officer,
"just as I thought. It's that fool Bock again.
Starting a scare just before the Führer's arrival
to attract attention to himself. That's the S.S. all

over. They must always discover plots and spies to show themselves more efficient than the *Abwehr*."

"Don't worry, sir," replied the other officer soothingly. "The escaped prisoners are too busy getting out of the area, thanks to the S.S., to bother with sabotage. All this talk of English spies is to direct attention from Bock's own mismanagement of the prisoners."

Schieffen nodded.

"That is so," he agreed. "Nevertheless, when the control practice is finished I want a guard posted on each floor continually until the operation starts. Delacroix, go and inform Captain Heffer what I want." He glanced at Sherwood. "This man is helping you?"

"He has been opening the guns for my inspection, *Herr Kolonel*," replied Delacroix smartly.

Schieffen nodded again. "Carry on, then. You will be on duty on this floor after the practice, Delacroix. Remind Captain Heffer, I want only Abwehr men on guard duty. Is that clear?"

"Yes, *Herr Kolonel*."

"Hurry, then. The practice starts in a few minutes—and Delacroix——" the Colonel's cold face lit up with a thin smile, "—I think you may be told now: To-night the Führer arrives and Project 38 goes into action at last!"

Delacroix stared at him blankly for a moment, then pushed Sherwood into a waiting lift and pressed a button marked "Control Floor." There were twelve floors indicated on the panel. He mopped the perspiration from his face, which had turned very pale, as they dropped smoothly downwards.

"No questions, Sherwood," he murmured, "Just follow me."

The lift stopped and opened on to a much larger and busier hall which had several sets of double swing-doors down one side. A green light glowed on the wall. Sentries were inspecting the passes of white-overalled technicians filing through the doors.

Delacroix pushed his way to the head of the queue, with Sherwood close behind.

"Make way!" shouted Delacroix, waving a pass. "Security! Security! Let me get through!"

"Hi!" shouted the sentry, pointing at Sherwood. "Where's this chap's pass?"

"He's with me," snapped Delacroix, "the security phone's out of order. It must be repaired."

"The S.S. have posted orders that only men with passes . . ." began the sentry.

"Never mind the S.S. These are Colonel Schieffen's orders," snarled Delacroix and barged through the double doors, shoving Sherwood on ahead.

Sherwood needed no telling that they were now in the control centre, the heart of Project 38. It was a vast hall, with a low, domed ceiling and sloping floor like a theatre. Five rows of control panels arranged in groups of about twenty ran from end to end. They faced a platform on which desks, in the form of a half-circle, overlooked a plotting-table about fifty feet square.

"I must report to Captain Heffer," Delacroix murmured over his shoulder. "I will show you the security phone. Pretend to check it." He led the way along the control panel, at which the technicians were taking their places, towards the platform. He indicated a bright red telephone on one of the desks and leaving Sherwood, went over to a group of officers.

Sherwood tried to look as though he were testing the cable and at the same time edged round the desk to get a better view of what was on the plotting-table. It was a huge relief map of London.

He was still staring at it when Delacroix called him.

"Is the phone working? We must leave. The practice is about to start."

Just as they had reached the farther end of the hall, bells shrilled and everyone jumped to attention as a short, white-haired man in general's uniform came through a door at the back of the platform.

The last thing Sherwood saw before they passed out into a short corridor, was a blaze of arc lights coming on over the plotting-table.

"This is the security wing," said Delacroix, opening the door of a small office. "We shall be undisturbed until the practice is finished. No movement about the installation is permitted until it is over." He sat down heavily, mopping his forehead, and waving vaguely to a chair.

"Well, Sherwood, I suppose you want an explanation."

This was a prize understatement. Sherwood still half-believed that it was all some cat-and-mouse-game—that Delacroix would suddenly reveal his colours as a collaborator and German agent. He stared doubtfully at the flabby features and was met with a regard which was both hard and shrewd. Delacroix shook his head, as if denying Sherwood's silent accusation and said, rather wearily: "I know what you think but you are wrong, Sherwood. When the Germans occupied Belgium I offered to collaborate with them, but this was a cover for my activities with the Resistance. I gained much valuable information in this way. Later I met Schieffen and he gave me the chance of becoming an *Abwehr* agent, which I accepted gladly. I knew this would give me access to more important military information."

"Why didn't you tell us about Project 38, then?"

"I knew nothing about it," replied Delacroix impatiently. "There was something else I did not know. Schieffen had recruited me because he wanted to send me to England as a Belgian refugee, to work for him there."

"And you did that, too—all for the Resistance?" Sherwood interrupted. This was becoming too good to be true!

Delacroix smiled faintly. "Did you know that Colonel Nicholson was at Scotland Yard before the war? I, too, was in the Police here in Belgium. I knew him well. We worked together on several International Police Commissions. When I 'escaped' to England I went straight to him. He welcomed my help. As an agent of the *Abwehr* I was in a good position to assist with one of his worst problems—finding out how so many British agents were being trapped in Belgium and Holland."

"That was going to be a bit difficult if you were in England, wasn't it?" Sherwood asked, impressed but not yet convinced.

"A good question. To be of use I had to return to Belgium, but without arousing Schieffen's suspicions. It was for this purpose the affair at Hampstead was staged."

"Staged? Are you telling me that was a put-up job?"

"Colonel Nicholson arranged that I should be 'discovered' but allowed to escape back to Belgium. That way I should be no further use to the Germans in England. It worked, too, except that Merridew was too quick. He almost killed me. Even that turned out well. It convinced the Germans that I was one of them."

"Did Merridew know about you?"

Delacroix shook his head.

"Neither of you was told so that you could not betray me if you were captured. Bock can be very persuasive. Remember little Lepic?"

Sherwood remembered!

"I knew about *you*," Delacroix went on, "but then I had to know about British agents if I were to do my job."

"That would have been useful if the Germans had tumbled to you." Sherwood persisted, determined not to give way. He still could not lose the idea that a trap was being prepared, although he could not guess the purpose.

Delacroix was silent and motionless for a few seconds, then he held up his hand. Between his thumb and forefinger was a grey pellet.

"I always carry this. It will kill a man in

minutes. No, Sherwood, I would not have betrayed you." For all his grossness, Delacroix had dignity as he said it.

"I knew no more of Project 38 than you did when I returned to Belgium," he continued. "I knew nothing until Schieffen said, quite casually, that within a few weeks England would be destroyed and the war finished. I knew then that I had to drop my intelligence work and come here. It was not difficult to persuade Schieffen to bring me because I have been very useful to him in his troubles with the S.S. I knew you would need my help again."

"Again?"

Delacroix shrugged impatiently. "I saved you from discovery in the brewery, and again at the café, and if I had not blown up the 88-mm. gun yesterday, you would not be alive now. Do you still not believe me?"

Sherwood looked at him blankly. "I believe you," he replied at length, feeling rather foolish—and they had thought that Delacroix was a blunderer! "But how can we get out of here and send a message to London? They must know of this at once."

Delacroix shook his head. "You still do not understand. It is too late for messages. You heard what Schieffen said—Hitler will arrive in a few hours and Project 38 will go into action. By

to-morrow morning, Sherwood, there will scarcely be anyone left alive in London!"

Sherwood stared disbelievingly. "That's ridiculous! Even a hundred guns like this couldn't
destroy London in a night."

"I didn't say that. I said scarcely anyone would
be left alive. Only half the rockets are high
explosive. They are to create confusion; the rest
carry a liquefied poison gas. It is completely
deadly, Sherwood. Civilian gas-masks are useless."

"The yellow tanks outside?" asked Sherwood,
as the truth dawned on him.

"Everything connected with the gas is painted
yellow. They are reserve supplies outside."
Delacroix started to pace the room nervously.
"Even that is not all. The missiles are fired
vertically and when they reach maximum height
the rocket-motors take over under the control of
signals from the wireless masts you must have
seen. The target can be changed simply by alter-
ing the radio beams. No part of Britain is safe.
All the great centres of population can be wiped
out, one after another, long before the R.A.F. can
destroy the installation by bombing."

Sherwood felt completely crushed by the
magnitude of the threat which Delacroix had uncovered. The only clear thought he had was that
Colonel Nicholson had been more right than they

had dreamed in saying this might be the most important secret of the war.

"What can we do?" he demanded desperately.

Delacroix sank back into his chair, shaking his head until his heavy features trembled like jelly.

"I don't know, Sherwood. It would require a regiment of demolition experts to destroy this installation. It is beyond one or two men. In this situation I am a fish out of water."

Sherwood automatically put his hand to the bulge which Merridew's explosive fountain-pens were making in his jacket. It was an impossibly tall order unless . . . "The magazines where the rockets are stored . . .?"

"If that were possible, even I could have done something," Delacroix interrupted bitterly, "but only Schieffen can get in there, apart from a few technicians who are known personally to the guards. The guns are fed mechanically. Everything is controlled from the centre on this floor. The conveyor-belts run straight up from the magazines to the fusing galleries and then up again to the gun-chambers. It is all automatic, Sherwood. The first rockets are already waiting at the fusing galleries."

A bell in the corridor rang three times and, as though it were a signal, Sherwood saw in that moment what they had to do.

Delacroix stood up wearily as though admitting defeat: "That is the end of the final practice. The next time the bell rings will be for Project 38 to go into operation. I thought there would be more time . . ."

Sherwood caught his arm. "The conveyors—can they be worked individually?"

Delacroix looked at him searchingly before replying. "For maintenance they can be worked from control panels, in the magazines, and in the fusing galleries. But why, Sherwood—what are you thinking?"

"We must get up to a fusing gallery before Schieffen's security guard is posted," Sherwood snapped decisively. "I'll explain as we go."

The technicians were already filing out of the control centre, and no one bothered with them as they hurried through to the lifts. Sherwood felt his heart pounding with excitement as they stood watching the indicator lights flicker. He knew that everything now depended on whether they could find out how to work a conveyor. If they could just keep one moving long enough to carry a rocket back down to the magazine, and if Merridew's "fountain-pens" would set it off when it got there, there was a chance—a faint chance—that they could detonate the magazines.

"Anything," wheezed Delacroix when Sher-

wood had explained, "anything is worth trying."

The first fusing gallery was deserted and there
was no sign yet of the security guard.

"Wedge the lift open—we shall need it again in a
hurry," said Delacroix. "We'll try here."

He scurried along the gallery to the nearest
chamber. Sherwood guessed that it was here the
final adjustments to the rockets would be carried
out to make the warheads live. The steel-link
conveyor ran up in an open vertical shaft through
floor and ceiling to the gun-chamber immediately
above. There was just room for one man to
squeeze beside the mechanism standing by
the conveyor, ready to fuse the first rocket, the
yellow nose of which projected above the floor
level.

"No good," muttered Delacroix. "That one is
filled with gas. We want a high explosive one,
with a red cap."

Sherwood found what they wanted in the third
chamber, while Delacroix hurried on ahead to
locate the control panel which would operate the
conveyor independently of the main system.
Sherwood had laid the "fountain-pens" out on the
floor and was looking round for something to
fix them to the rocket with, when Delacroix returned.

"Here—use this, Sherwood," he said, stripping

off his tie. "Then come to the panel. I do not see how it works."

Sherwood knotted the tie in a loop and clipped on the "fountain-pens." It just fitted over the tip of the red nose-cap—but only just.

"Have you set them?" demanded Delacroix anxiously.

"Not yet. We must make sure we can work the conveyor first."

It had just occurred to Sherwood that he had no idea how long the "fountain-pens" would take to explode after they had been set. The ones Merridew had used on Jeanmaire's shop had been almost instantaneous. He had said that these would take longer, but not how much longer. Sherwood decided that there was no point in thinking about it.

He joined Delacroix at the panel, which was about ten yards away, in an alcove off the gallery. A quick glance at the controls showed that they were not complicated. White arrowheads beside the switches clearly referred to upwards and downwards movements of the conveyor, while green and red crosses suggested stopping and starting. There was also a lever with a dial beside it, which he guessed was for regulating the speed.

"You stay here," he said to Delacroix. "I'm going back to the chamber. When I give the word, throw this switch with the down arrow against it.

Directly the conveyor starts moving, I'll set the 'pens.' Then we'll make a dash for the lift."

Delacroix nodded. "How long shall we have to get clear?"

"I don't know—not long."

Delacroix nodded again. "No matter. It will be worth it."

Sherwood slipped back to the chamber, leaned over the fusing mechanism and caught hold of the first "pen." If one or two were set properly they would be enough to explode the rest. The two lines which had to meet were just visible.

"Right!" he called.

There was a loud click from the control panel, but the conveyor did not budge. He waited for a few seconds and then went out to see what had happened. Delacroix was staring angrily at the panel.

"It does not work. What can be wrong, Sherwood?"

Sherwood could have kicked himself for not thinking of it earlier.

"There must be a master-switch which cuts out the control centre and brings this panel into operation."

"This one," suggested Delacroix, pointing to a big lever-switch beneath the panel.

Sherwood neutralised the down control.

"Try it," he said.

Delacroix eased it down and at once a warning light came on at the top of the panel. "That's it, Sherwood. We must try again. Hurry!"

As Sherwood started back to the chamber a figure in field-grey appeared at the end of the gallery. The security guard had arrived. His voice echoed angrily along the gallery.

"You! What are you doing? This floor is supposed to be cleared."

There was no time to argue.

"Now!" yelled Sherwood desperately.

The conveyor jerked and started to move slowly downwards. He had set four of the "pens" and was reaching for the fifth when there was a series of deafening explosions. For a second he thought the "pens" had gone off instantaneously, then he saw the body of the security guard spread-eagled on the floor of the gallery. The man did not move as Sherwood jumped over him and ran to the alcove. Delacroix was leaning heavily against the wall, a revolver dangling by his side. On the floor lay the shattered levers of the master-switch and stop-control.

"They can't do anything about it now," groaned Delacroix. "You must leave me, I've been hit. It is bad—I know it is bad."

Sherwood put his shoulder under the Belgian's arm and half dragged, half carried him along the gallery.

The lift had gone. The guard must have thought the door was jammed and released it.

He propped Delacroix, who was now scarcely conscious, against the wall and pressed all the call buttons. Almost at once a door slid open, which seemed too good to be true until Schieffen stepped out. The German stiffened, his white face more mask-like than ever.

"What is this?"

Delacroix groaned and opened his eyes.

"Quickly—a saboteur, Herr Kolonel . . . fusing chamber . . .!"

"Take him down," snapped Schieffen to Sherwood. "Tell Captain Heffer to report here with six men at once." He ran off down the gallery as Sherwood dragged Delacroix into the lift and pressed the bottom button. Delacroix slumped against the side with his eyes closed again. His grey face and noisy breathing showed how badly he was wounded, but there was no sign of blood on him.

The lift seemed desperately slow. Too slow to beat the acid eating through the "fountain-pen" fuses. Sherwood broke into a cold sweat just thinking about them. He knew that if they reached the bottom alive they still had to get out through the guarded entrance to the open, and Delacroix did not look as if he could make it.

Delacroix solved that problem himself, however, when at last the door slid back. They had come down into one of the entrance halls through which a rail spur passed. It was in semi-darkness, but to their right, about twenty yards away, was a brightly lit guard-room covering the entrance. The sentries were outside, more concerned with anyone entering than leaving, but it could be only a matter of minutes before they were alerted by a general alarm.

Delacroix put his arm round Sherwood's neck and staggered out of the lift. The cold air blowing revived him a bit.

"Call the guard, Sherwood," he croaked. "Leave the talking to me."

Sherwood shouted several times before one of the guards came running.

"What's going on?" he demanded. "What are you doing here?"

Delacroix waved him aside.

"It's the heat in there," he muttered. "It upset me. Let me get some fresh air. I'll be all right."

The sentry, a beefy, bull-necked type, stood back contemptuously. "You're too fat," he jeered. "You can't hang around here. The Führer's train has been signalled a few miles down the line. You'd better clear off out of sight."

Sherwood could feel the man's eyes on their backs as they swayed out through the entrance.

"I shan't let you in again if you haven't got your passes," he called after them, as a parting shot.

Delacroix dragged himself along until they were through the patch of light at the entrance and out into the darkness. He was staggering so much Sherwood could hardly keep him up.

"You leave me, Sherwood," he whispered. "I can't go any farther."

He was clearly speaking the truth, so Sherwood looked round for a way to support him. About fifty yards off to the left in the unloading area, an unattended diesel was ticking over. If he could get Delacroix aboard they might be able to crash through the control-point out into the ravine, where, with luck, Merridew and Krunjes would now be waiting.

Leaving Delacroix doubled up on the ground, he raced along the track, reaching the engine without being seen. The driver was standing on the farther side reading a paper under one of the lights. He looked up and opened his mouth as Sherwood jumped into the cab to release the brake, but what he shouted was drowned by a burst of firing.

Over his shoulder, Sherwood saw Colonel Schieffen with a squad of men at his heels, streaming from the entrance, shooting wildly at the engine. They did not see Delacroix until he lurched up out of the darkness, straight in front of them, shouting and firing his revolver.

Just for an instant the surprise attack halted them, and in that instant the ground began trembling.

Like the approach of an express train, with each shock wave more violent than the last, a massive commotion roared up out of the earth, until it seemed to reach the surface, then the whole hill containing the Project erupted. Sherwood had a fleeting glimpse of Delacroix and Schieffen in the path of a great flame that burst from the entrance to sweep across the compound, setting the trees beyond on fire.

Then they were gone.

The searing blast shattered the windows of the cab as he fell back shielding his face. Far above, the muzzles of the guns spouted fire and yellow smoke like nightmare fountains. The sides of the hill caved in and poured downwards in devastating landslides, engulfing the store buildings and tanks at the foot. Rock fragments whistled down through the smoke, making the cab of the diesel ring as though it were being bombarded with shell splinters.

He was shoved roughly aside and saw the chalk-white face of the driver above him. The man wrenched frantically at the controls, sending the engine bucketing towards the check-point. As Sherwood dragged himself up he saw that the driver was pointing at the dense yellow smoke rolling down the hill towards them like a flood and realised that this must be the poison gas intended for England. It blotted out the hill, giving an unearthly light to the raging fires beneath.

Yellow tongues licked across the ground and by the time the engine hit the check-point were lapping over the footplate. The demented driver jammed the throttle wide open, crashing through the barrier out into the ravine.

Several times Sherwood thought they were coming off the rails and, directly the solitary rock, marking the rendezvous with Merridew and Krunjes, came into view, standing out starkly in the yellow light, he grabbed the brake and flung it over. The driver tried to drag him away, but he hung on. After one last desperate effort, the man hurled himself, screaming, out of the cab, clawing for a hold on the steep side of the ravine.

Sherwood swung himself out and up on to the roof and without waiting for the engine to come to a halt, leap across to the edge of the cutting and crashed his way upwards through the brush.

Merridew was waiting half-way across the slope. He had seen the diesel approaching with a figure clinging to the top, and had come running down towards the track. Sherwood could not hear what Merridew was shouting, still being deaf from the explosion. He did not know at the time, but he had also lost most of his hair in the scorching blast that had killed Delacroix and Schieffen; but for the moment none of this mattered as they scrambled together up towards the rock to join Krunjes, who was gazing open-mouthed at the holocaust raging behind them.

Krunjes's greeting was almost as violent as the explosion had been, and he still had one last surprise to spring on the now exhausted Sherwood.

In the shadow of the boulder lay the wretched Bock, dishevelled and hog-tied. It had been he who had discovered Merridew and Krunjes while they were lowering Sherwood into the gun. After a running gun-fight they had turned the tables and having captured him, forced him to escort them out through the check-point to the forest. Krunjes solved the problem of disposing of him by carrying him down to the diesel and sending it coasting towards the railhead.

"A present for the Führer," Krunjes explained later.

While he was doing this, Merridew and Sherwood stood looking back at Project 38. A pall of

smoke and gas had spread over the hill, reflecting
down the uncanny yellow light on to the inferno
below. From time to time the ground shuddered
as the flames found secondary stores of explosives.
Sherwood thought of old Lepic and Delacroix
and wished that they too could have been there
to see how their courage and sacrifice had been
justified.

Merridew pulled his arm and they turned to
follow Krunjes, who was already hurrying up the
slope into the cover of the forest.

*   *   *   *

There their mission ended and little remains to
tell. Thanks to Krunjes's knowledge of the
country, they got away into France, where they
were hidden by the *Maquis*. Eventually Merridew
and Sherwood passed along one of the organised
escape routes across France into Spain. From
there the British embassy laid on a special flight
back to England.

Krunjes stayed on to fight with the *Maquis* and
they did not see him again until the war was over;
then they had a reunion at Dinant and revisited
the site of Project 38.

It was just as the Germans had abandoned it—
a desolate blackened ruin, but in front of the
shattered entrance through which Sherwood had

escaped, the Belgian Government had erected a plain stone block with this inscription:

ON THIS SPOT
DIED
RAOUL DELACROIX
21ST FEBRUARY, 1944.
A SOLDIER AND A PATRIOT